*Under his stroking hands,
Casey's body went slack, surrendering
to sheer sensuality . . .*

Her arms went up around his neck, her fingers twisted in his rough black hair. She wondered wildly what had come over her to make her shake off, so easily, her qualms about making careless love without commitment. Hungrily, blindly, she sought his mouth, her kiss conveying a deep-buried heat within her own body about to flare out of control. One night out of a lifetime isn't too much to ask, she thought. Then desire flooded her mind, obliterating all reason.

WHAT ARE *LOVESWEPT* ROMANCES?

They are stories of true romance and touching emotion. We believe those two very important ingredients are constants in our highly sensual and very believable stories in the *LOVESWEPT* line. Our goal is to give you, the reader, stories of consistently high quality that may sometimes make you laugh, sometimes make you cry, but are always fresh and creative and contain many delightful surprises within their pages.

Most romance fans read an enormous number of books. Those they truly love, they keep. Others may be traded with friends and soon forgotten. We hope that each *LOVESWEPT* romance will be a treasure—a "keeper." We will always try to publish

LOVE STORIES YOU'LL NEVER FORGET
BY AUTHORS YOU'LL ALWAYS REMEMBER

The Editors

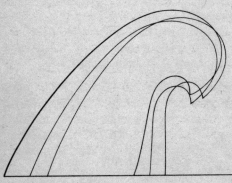

LOVESWEPT · 6

Dorothy Garlock

A Love for All Time

BANTAM BOOKS · TORONTO · NEW YORK · LONDON · SYDNEY

A LOVE FOR ALL TIME
A Bantam Book / May 1983

*LOVESWEPT and the wave device are trademarks of
Bantam Books, Inc.*

ISBN 0-553-21606-6

Published simultaneously in the United States and Canada

---

*Bantam Books are published by Bantam Books, Inc. Its
trademark, consisting of the words "Bantam Books" and the
portrayal of a rooster, is Registered in U.S. Patent and Trademark Office and in other countries. Marca Registrada. Bantam
Books, Inc., 666 Fifth Avenue, New York, New York 10103.*

PRINTED IN THE UNITED STATES OF AMERICA

O   0 9 8 7 6 5 4 3 2 1

One

Someone was crying.

The sounds were so soft that at first Casey wasn't sure what she was hearing. They were coming at quick intervals, with intermittent panicky little gasps.

"Is someone there?" *Was that her voice?* It was muffled and strange.

The crying grew louder. Casey's mind groped its way into full awareness. Curiosity gave way to fright when she realized the sobs were coming from her own throat. She lifted a hand to her face. It didn't hurt; it only felt . . . heavy. And her mouth was dry, her tongue clinging to the roof. She tried to turn her head, but movement was impossible. *If she was awake, why couldn't she see?* Nothing seemed to make sense.

"Are my eyes open?" she asked aloud, forcing her tongue to make the necessary movements.

"I can't see!" The words were anguished. Panic, then terror seized her.

"Shhh . . . Lie still." The voice was deep, masculine and muffled. "Don't be frightened. You can't see because there's a bandage over your eyes."

The calm words drew her back from the brink of hysteria.

"You're in the hospital, but you'll be all right."

"But . . . I can't see!"

"The doctor said the bandage can come off soon," the calm voice persisted. "You've a concussion and must keep your head still." Hands held her forearms gently. "Keep your arms still, too. You're taking fluids intravenously." He moved her arms gently to her sides and kept his hands there.

"Why . . . what . . .?" She tried to sniff and something large and soft was dabbed to her nose.

"You were in an accident. The doctor will be here soon. He can tell you about your injuries. Don't be frightened. I . . ." The voice seemed to move away.

"Don't leave me!" She tried to lift her arms, but they were gently forced down.

"I won't leave you. I'll keep my hand on your arm so you'll know I'm here."

"Oh, I remember! I was on the highway. The fog—"

"Don't think about it now."

But she did. It all came rushing back. She remembered her own voice screaming in her ears and then the endless shattering of glass and the . . . crunching, metal grinding . . . breaking, tearing and cracking. Then everything stopped and the world turned black.

"Oh, dear God! Was . . . anyone killed?" The words came with fresh sobs.

"No one was killed." The voice was smooth and quiet. The handkerchief came to her nose again. "You mustn't cry." Then with an attempt at humor, "until you can wipe your own nose."

"I'm thirsty."

"I'll see about getting you a drink. Will you be frightened if I leave you?" The hand on her arm tightened just a fraction.

"Don't go!"

"I won't be gone any longer than it takes you to count to twenty. I promise."

The hand left her arm and she strained her ears to hear him open the door, but it must have been ajar. *One, two, three, four, five* . . . Then a voice, low, controlled and icy. She forgot about counting.

"What the hell do you mean leaving her alone? Dammit! She woke up scared to death!"

"I was only gone for a few minutes." This voice was trembly and feminine.

"You were hired to stay with her." The calm voice was no longer calm. It was angry and censorious.

"I'm sorry—"

"Being sorry isn't enough. Get the doctor in here. She needs some answers. *And*," he added with a touch of menace to his tone, "she's thirsty."

"She can have water sparingly."

"I'll do that while you get the doctor."

There was a small silence and then Casey felt the hand on her arm again.

"Cassandra?"

"Casey. Everyone calls me Casey."

"All right, Casey. You can have some water. I'll give it to you while the nurse goes for the doctor. I'm going to put the end of the tube in the corner of your mouth. Take only a small amount at a time until you see how it goes down." The man's voice was low pitched and even tenored as if nothing could move him to anger, but something had— that nurse abandoning her post.

The water was cold and good, but it was too much of an effort to draw it into her mouth. The tube was removed and she licked her lips with the tip of her tongue.

"There's a small ice cube here. Do you want to hold it in your mouth?"

"Yes, please," she whispered, tired now.

"Be careful and don't let it slip down your throat."

She parted her lips and a sliver of ice was placed between them. It was so small it disappeared almost at once, but left a coolness in her mouth.

"Are you a doctor?"

"No. My name's Dan."

Casey felt a flash of disappointment, and then another voice reached her ears.

"Good evening." The warm hand left her arm. "Miss Farrow, I'm Dr. Masters."

"Please take the bandage off my eyes!" she blurted out desperately.

"Not until tomorrow. There's a cut across your forehead and your eyelids are swollen." The voice was calm and impersonal, not at all as warm as the other man's. "You must lie very still for another twenty-four hours. I'll give you something to make you sleep."

"No! What's wrong with me? My hands are bandaged, too. And I feel numb all over. I can't feel my legs! Oh, God! Are my legs on?" Panic made her voice shrill.

"They sure are, and you've enough stitches in them for a patchwork quilt," he said lightly.

"I don't believe you! Where's that man? Please . . . man! Where are you?"

"I'm here, Casey." The now familiar voice came from the other side of the bed and his hand encircled her forearm. "The doctor's telling the truth. The cuts had to be stitched, but other than that your legs are all right."

"Is there any pain?" the doctor asked.

"No, everything is numb." A fresh sob came from her throat. "I've got to know . . . about my face!"

"Tell her!" Dan's voice grated and his fingers tightened on her arm. "She's got a right to know."

Another sob broke from the bandages.

"Miss Farrow! Miss Farrow!" The doctor said again in a louder, sterner voice. "Calm down or I'll give you a sedative. I won't lie to you about your injuries. You have a deep cut down the side of your face. You covered your face with your hands and protected it, all but the right side. In time we can fix it so scarcely a scar remains. You also have several broken ribs and a concussion."

"But . . . why am I all bandaged?" She tried to lift her hand toward the man called Dan.

"Your car crashed into the back of a truck carrying a load of windows. The tail of the truck smashed right through your windshield. Only a few inches more and the rear of the truck would have crushed you. As it was, you were showered with flying glass." His hand was firm on her arm and his voice quietly confident. "The cuts have been stitched and you have been given something to kill the pain, that's the reason your body feels numb."

"The best thing for you is sleep," the doctor said. He moved aside and made room for the nurse with the hypodermic syringe. She lifted Casey's arm, shook her head, and lowered it when she couldn't find a place to give the injection amid the network of puckered cuts held together with surgical stitches. She looked inquiringly at the doctor and he carefully lifted the sheet to expose a section of thigh. The nurse bent and quickly injected the needle.

"I'm hoping to take the bandage off your eyes tomorrow." The doctor talked calmly while he looked at the hundreds of cuts on her thighs and legs. It had taken him almost six hours to pick the glass out of her flesh and close the wounds on her beautiful body. What would her reaction be when she looked at it for the first time? He shook his gray head. She would have to live with the results of the accident for a long time, but at that, she was lucky to be alive.

"M . . . an, are you still here?" Casey's voice was slurred as she fought to stay awake.

"Dan." The comforting voice was close to her. "You'll not be left alone, Casey. Go to sleep."

"How . . . long have I been here?"

"Almost twenty-four hours. I notified your father and he'll be coming to see you in a few days."

"How . . . did . . . ?"

"I got his name and address from your employer and called him." He gently stroked the one place on her forearm that was free of cuts and scratches. "You're not to worry. Everything has been taken care of."

"But . . . who are you?"

Casey struggled to stay awake to hear the answer to her question, but the drug she had been given took effect and she slid into a deep, engulfing abyss.

She was swimming up out of the murky darkness. She wanted to sleep, but she was being lifted, turned, and she tried to push the punishing hands from her tortured body. Someone lifted her legs and she cried out. There was a sharp tug on her hair and she cried out again. At last she was allowed to lie back and was covered with something soft. Soothing words calmed and reassured her. A strong, rough hand stroked her arm. Her heart settled into a quieter pace as the pain subsided and finally her sleep deepened and the nightmare left her.

The sensation of something against her mouth woke her abruptly. She felt as if a thousand needles pierced her flesh, and she couldn't hold back the little gasp of pain that came up out of her dry throat. The whole side of her face throbbed in almost unbearable pain with every beat of her heart, and her eyelids seemed to be glued shut. It took a supreme effort to open them a mere crack. She saw the shape of a window, the shade partly drawn. She began to cry. Tears rolled down the side of her nose and across her mouth.

Through the blur of tears she saw a bottle hanging upside down beside the bed with tubes running to her arm. She turned her head slightly. A white-caped nurse was bending over her.

"Awake at last!" The voice was young, cheerful. "Is your mouth dry? I've been wetting your lips with a damp cloth."

Casey opened her mouth to speak, but no words came out. She tried again and managed to say, "Water."

A glass tube was placed in her mouth. She puckered her lips around it. The water was delicious, cool, and she could feel it streaming through her body. The tube was removed and Casey opened her eyes wider. The nurse smiled at her. She was pretty. Very pretty. She'd make a good model for cosmetic demonstrations, Casey thought dully, her skin's clear and smooth.

"What time is it?" she asked, and lifted her hand to look at the watch she usually wore. The thing she lifted, the drawn, clawlike thing, with the dark spikes of surgical thread studding it, couldn't be *her* hand! The long, tapered nails were cut bluntly, the polish removed, the fingers curled as if she were holding an invisible egg. "Oh!" she gasped and tried to lift her other hand, but the nurse reached across to press it firmly to the bed.

"It's two o'clock. I'm going off duty soon. We can get acquainted before I leave."

Casey stared stupidly at the nurse, fear making her speechless. Her hands were ruined! The long, slender fingers that held a bottle of scent for the television commercials; the smooth fingers that glided cream over the faces of hundreds of beautiful models during demonstrations for Allure Cosmetics, looked like the fingers of an old crone, a witch!

Instantly she became aware of her body lying naked beneath the sheet. Whimpering, she tried to lift the covering. Her hand clawed frantically as she pressed her chin to her chest so she could look down at her body.

"I've got to see! Please . . ."

"Of course you do." The nurse's voice was patronizing. "Just lie still. You're healing nicely." She lifted the sheet. "The doctor used as few dressings as possible and the sheets are sterile. He did a wonderful job . . ."

The nurse's chatter fell on deaf ears. Casey looked at the bandages on her breast and at the hundreds of cuts that covered her stomach, hips and thighs. Her pulse leaped convulsively and she raised imploring eyes to the nurse.

"I'm . . . cut all over!" she gasped. She lifted her free hand and felt the bandage on her face. "Is it very bad?" she whispered.

"It's a big dressing," the nurse said lightly. "Doctors are notorious for bulky dressings. The rest of your face is perfect, not a scratch."

"I don't believe you! I want to see it." Casey's voice rose in panic. Dread lay heavy within her.

"I don't have a mirror. You'll have to take my word for it. Dr. Masters will be in to see you soon and no doubt Mr. Murdock will be here, too. Would you like more water?"

Casey closed her eyes and turned her face away. Tears rolled from beneath her swollen lids and wet the pillow beneath her cheek. She felt old, broken, as though her life had come to an end. How could she possibly conduct a beauty seminar with a scarred face and hands? She'd spent seven years with Allure Cosmetics and was one of their top consultants. Neil Hamilton, her boss and president of the company, was a perfectionist. He'd told her many times it was her flawless complexion, her poise and confidence that made her so much in demand as a demonstrator.

Life had been a struggle ever since she could remember. Her father and mother had divorced when she was small, and her mother died suddenly when she was a senior in high school. After that it had been one job after another until she went to work in the cosmetic section of a large department store. It was while working there that she came in contact with Allure beauty products. Now seven years later she was back to square one, but this time with a handicap.

Casey never had a great opinion of herself, but others admired her for her sweet nature, her sturdy personality and her beauty. Tall, five foot nine, and willowy, she wore her heavy honey-gold hair in a loose, casual style reaching to shoulder length. Her eyebrows and lashes were naturally darker, and her eyes a clear tawny gold harmonizing with her hair. Her face was a perfect oval with a small fine nose and full soft lips. Casey knew the contentment of being satisfied with herself.

Her father came back into her life four years ago and any resentment she felt toward him for not being there when she was young faded when she realized he was a weaker, less secure person than she, for all his handsome, gallant ways. A handsome rogue. That's the way she thought of him, and it was no wonder her mother had loved him so desperately.

"Miss Farrow . . . are you all right?"

"Yes. Yes, I'm all right." Casey tried to sound more "all right" than she was.

"You're coming along nicely. The doctor did a wonderful job putting you back together."

Casey rolled her head on the pillow. She looked

frightened and helpless, but resentful, too. "Please don't tell me that again. I'm sure the doctor did his best."

Later the young nurse with the peachy complexion left and a fat matronly woman took her place. The tubes were removed from Casey's arm and the bottle rolled out of sight. Casey lay quietly, her thoughts as painful as her injuries. What would she do? Would there be a position available at Allure that didn't require meeting the public? She knew nothing about office work. Demonstrating was her field. Would Neil employ her now that she was no longer a walking advertisement for his company?

The doctor came in and stood at the foot of the bed. He wore a gown and a mask dangled from a cord around his neck. His eyes looked kindly behind horn-rimmed glasses.

"Hello. I'm Dr. Masters."

"You're the one who did the wonderful job." The words rolled out and Casey was surprised at how bitter she sounded.

"Not exactly wonderful, but we did get all the holes closed." The doctor sounded merciless, and Casey hated him. He moved around to the side of the bed and sat down. The nurse silently left the room.

"I've asked for a mirror, but they won't give me one." Her eyes were full of tears again. She couldn't seem to stop crying.

"You won't be able to see anything until I remove the dressing in a few days. I'll tell you anything you want to know."

"How . . . bad is it?" They were the hardest words she ever had to say.

"It could be much worse. I just told a young woman her leg's coming off in the morning and a father of two that he won't live to see his third child born." Casey turned her face away. The doctor sighed. "You have a deep laceration that starts at the hairline above your right eye and curves around the side of your face. Part of the flesh was cut away, and . . . a good part of your right ear lobe. . . ." Casey rolled her head toward him and an endless sob burst from her. "It will be a few months before any more work can be done. But, it's my opinion that a specialist in plastic surgery will be able to repair your face and ear." The doctor sounded firm and impersonal.

"And the . . . rest of me?" Casey had to know. "My hands?"

"You'll have full use of your hands. No tendons were cut."

"But the scars . . ."

"They'll fade a great deal in time."

Casey realized there was a different look in his eyes. He was impatient with her. But dammit! He used his hands to make a living, the same as she did!

"You probably think I'm vain, Doctor, but my hands and face are important in my line of work. I'm a demonstrator for a cosmetic firm and . . ." She couldn't say it. She couldn't say aloud that seven years of work had ended.

The doctor stood. "I understand, Miss Farrow." His eyes were kinder, now. "Mr. Murdock insisted we bring in Dr. Clemons, who comes well recommended as one of the top men in his field. You may want to talk to him about your breast. He—"

"My breast?"

"We did the best we could, but—"

"But, what?" The even tone of his voice was driving her crazy.

"It was cut deeply by the flying glass."

"Oh, God! Oh, God, what else?" Casey turned her head from side to side in a sharp frantic motion. She retched as though to throw up, but nothing came.

"You're very lucky to be alive. Murdock got you here just in time or you'd have bled to death." His voice was very professional, as if he was trying hard not to compare her loss with that of the girl who'd lose her leg in the morning.

"Thank you for telling me . . . everything," Casey said in a softly resigned voice. It didn't occur to her to ask about the man who saved her life. That thought would come to her later.

The lights in the room were dim. The nurse sat in the chair beside the door, quiet after Casey refused to be drawn into conversation. She had been given a pain pill, but refused the medication that would make her sleep. She had always been very health conscious. Good food, exercise and as few drugs as possible were the basis of her philosophy for keeping fit.

When the light tap on the door reached her, Casey didn't bother to turn her head. She had watched the sky gradually darken and now lights from the street below reflected on the window. That time of day between sundown and dusk was a depressing time of day for her. It was the time of day that families gathered. She had no family except Eddie, her father. He came and went with a constant succession of women, but she learned to turn a blind eye, realizing that neither they nor anything else meant more to him than the pleasure of the moment. The twilight hours signaled that the day was over. Casey hated the ending of anything.

The door closed softly. She turned her head. The nurse had stepped outside. Good. She had told her repeatedly during the last few hours that she didn't have to stay with her, but the woman had stated firmly that she had been instructed not to leave the room. Casey had responded with the fact that her insurance didn't cover private nursing. The woman had shrugged her heavy shoulders and refused to argue the point.

The door opened and Casey groaned inwardly. Her moments alone had been few. A man came into the room and closed the door behind him. Casey's eyes focused on the tall, dark-haired figure that came to stand beside the bed.

There was a curious silence as though neither of them knew what to say, he staring down at her, she up at him.

Casey slowly absorbed his height, his wide shoulders, the soft white, open-necked shirt tucked neatly into dark trousers. It was difficult for her to decide if he was handsome or not. He might have been, at one time, before he had done whatever it was that rearranged his features into the rugged, slightly battered pattern. His hair was nearly black and so were his eyes, a dark, dark gray—dark as flint Casey decided. They looked right into her as if to read her every thought. He looked more like a lumberjack than a doctor, yet he must be one.

"Are you the doctor who's going to put me back together?" she asked at last.

"No. I'm Dan Murdock."

The voice jerked her to attention before the name registered. This was the voice that soothed her, brought her back from panicsville when she awoke with her eyes bandaged. She lifted her large velvety tawny-gold eyes, the thick dark lashes curling back from them and leaving them very wide.

"Who are you?" she asked without inflection.

He looked at her thoughtfully. "May I sit down?"

She nodded, surprised that he asked. Her eyes followed him when he went to get the chair beside the door. He really was a monolith of a man, she thought. Everything about him fit perfectly—his voice, eyes, the way he moved.

He treaded softly across the room with the chair,

placed it beside the bed and eased his bulk down into it. He sat there, a knee crossed over, one booted foot swinging in her angle of vision. He was waiting with a patience that was deliberate, tangible.

"Are you going to tell me who you are?" Casey said in brittle tones. "No. Let me guess. You're my insurance adjuster."

"Wrong. I'm the man who ran into the back of your car and pushed it into the truck carrying windows." The gray eyes watched her for some sign of an emotional upheaval.

"What am I suppose to say? Thanks for ruining my life?" she said evenly.

"I want you to know, Casey, that I was driving carefully that night, and that I didn't see your car until seconds before I hit it. There must have been a cloud of dense fog that blotted out the taillights on your car."

"The fog was terribly thick," she said in a careful tone. "I was just creeping along." She had been warned to stay off the highway, but in spite of the warning she had driven down to Newberg to speak to a class graduating from beauty school. "It wasn't your fault. I shouldn't have been on the highway. But neither should you." Dammit! From the looks of him he'd come out of the accident without a scratch. Let him carry some of the blame.

"If one of us had used a little more sense the accident wouldn't have happened."

Casey looked at him and wondered if he had ever fought for anything. Had life given him all he wanted? She wished he would leave. Tears threatened to engulf her at any minute, but under his appraisal she refused to give in to them.

"Are you wondering if I'm going to sue you?" What had made her ask such a thing?

"I hadn't thought about it. Are you?"

Embarrassed, she closed her eyes for a moment, opened them and stared into his. "No." Tears slid down her cheeks and she was unable to stem the flood.

"Your father will be here in a day or two. I found him in Seattle. He'd have been here today, but the Seattle airport was fogged in."

"It was kind of you. Has my employer been notified?"

"Yes. I talked with him on the phone. He's leaving today for Los Angeles, but said he'd be in to see you as soon as he returns." Her lids flickered as she tried to regain her composure. "Your car was towed in, that is, what was left of it. I'm afraid there wasn't much to salvage. We were lucky to find your purse and identification."

"Why are you doing these things for me? You said the accident wasn't your fault." She stared with bewilderment at his hard-boned face. His eyes, half-veiled by heavy lids, stared back into hers.

"I'm doing it because I want to, Casey." His bluntness surprised her. She looked at him with new interest as he pulled a soft handkerchief out of his pocket and put it in her hand. "Can you manage?" he asked softly. His voice was so like the voice that had come out of the darkness to reassure her the night she came to after the accident that she almost cried again, but she didn't. She wiped her nose, holding the handkerchief clumsily. He took it from her hand. "Let me." He gently wiped her eyes, then her nose, and the tenderness of the gesture caused her to feel, for a moment . . . cherished.

"The doctor said you saved my life by bringing me to the hospital yourself. Thank you."

He smiled, his eyes faintly teasing. "You're welcome. Did he tell you that you have some of my blood in your veins? Luckily your blood type was on your identification card and it's the same as mine. It saved time."

"I'm doubly indebted to you," she murmured.

He bent over so that his face was close to hers. "No, Casey. I don't want you to feel as if you owe me a thing."

"But I do," she said in a whisper. "Thank you. I don't know what else to say."

"Don't say anything." His voice deepened, became husky, and his face turned serious. "I knew as soon as I lifted you out of the wreckage you were someone special to me. I want us to get to know each other, Casey." He stood and she thought again how tall he was. He would top her five foot nine frame by several inches. "I won't be back for a couple of days, but I'll keep in touch." His dark eyes held hers. "Do you believe in reincarnation?"

"I don't know," Casey said in a voice that quivered a little in spite of her attempt at control.

"I do. I believe we meant a lot to each other in another life and I mean for us to mean a lot to each other in this one."

He stood looking down at her while her mind tried to absorb the meaning of his words. A smile started in his dark eyes and spread to the rest of his face and then he bent and laid his lips gently against hers. There was nothing hesitant about his kiss, nothing tentative or uncertain. The pressure of his mouth was warm and firm, moving over her lips with familiar ease. When he raised his head he was still smiling.

"You're crazy!" Casey gasped through wobbly lips. "I don't know you . . . from Adam!"

He laughed. The sound was light and teasing and there was unmistakable admiration in his eyes.

"Somehow I knew you'd be like that." He laughed lightly again as if, suddenly, he was very happy. "You're not to worry about a thing. The doctors and nurses will take good care of you while I'm gone. Hurry and get well so you can get out of here."

Casey watched him leave. "He's not playing with a full deck," a voice, sounding strangely like her own, muttered.

Two

Casey felt as though someone had stuck a butcher knife in her chest and was slowly turning it. She had a strong desire to run from the image that faced her in the mirror, but her legs seemed disconnected from her body. She leaned forward and stared into gold-flecked eyes surrounded by bluish-green bruises, then, with deliberation, she studied the puckered ridge that crossed her forehead just an inch below the hairline and disappeared beneath the dressing on the side of her face. She closed her eyes and gripped the washbasin as she swayed. The pain in her hands when she gripped, and in her chest when she gasped, was nothing compared to the pain in her heart.

"Oh, God!" she murmured. "Am I such a shallow, vain person that I can't be thankful I'm alive?"

"Miss Farrow!" The nurse with the peachy complexion flung open the bathroom door. "You scared me to death! You shouldn't be out of bed."

Casey gritted her teeth. "I've lain in that bed for

five days. I'm not a child. I'm the one that's got to live with this face and I've got a right to look at it. Now, get out of here or I'll scream the place down!"

"I've talked to your doctor," the nurse said consolingly, "and we can shampoo your hair tomorrow. I know you'll feel better when you see how we can arrange it to cover . . . your forehead. Please, Miss Farrow, Mr. Murdock will be very angry if he finds out I've let you get out of bed."

"What the hell does he have to do with anything? He's just the man who ran into my car. I never set eyes on him before the accident." Casey was so immersed in her own misery she had to lash out at someone.

"I don't know anything about that," the nurse said firmly. "He's paying me to take care of you and that's what I'm going to do." Her voice softened. "I know how you feel, Miss Farrow." The girl's sympathy was apparent and would have embarrassed Casey had she the strength to feel such an emotion.

"You can't possibly know how I feel," Casey said crossly. "Beauty is my business! I'm supposed to be a walking advertisement for the products I sell. Look at my hands! They look like they've been through a meat grinder. Look at my face! I can cover up the rest of me, but not my face and hands!" Tears that came so easily rolled down her cheeks. "Oh, help me back to bed!" she muttered in despair.

Casey lay staring at the ceiling. She had never imagined that at age twenty-seven she could feel as though she had already lived a hundred years, that everything she had built her life around had collapsed in a heap. All that remained to be seen was if she had a position with the company at all. Neil had called from Los Angeles where he was opening a branch office. He told her that he would be back in Portland at the end of the week and would come to see her.

"I'm sorry you missed the regular conference," he had told her on the phone. "Exciting things are happening. You know that model I've been trying to get? Jennifer Carwilde? The one with the dark hair and the gorgeous skin? Well, I got her! She'll make a wonderful demonstrator. The girls will take one look at her and want to look just like her. Her skin is perfect. Not a blemish, not a single blemish . . ."

Not even foundation cream an inch thick would hide the blemishes on her skin, Casey thought with a fresh stab of self-pity. She lay silent, hugging her misery to her like a winter coat.

In the afternoon her father arrived with a huge bunch of flowers. In the short time Casey had known him she had become accustomed to the fact that her father never did anything in a small way. The bigger the better was Eddie Farrow's philosophy. Big car, big presents, big apartment, big bills he was always struggling to pay. He swaggered into the room with a big smile that turned into a big frown when he looked at his daughter.

"What the hell happened to you, cookie?"

There was a weakness, a vulnerability about her father that at times tore at Casey's heart. Eddie Farrow would never be able to stand on his own, therefore God gave him a glib tongue, a handsome face and body to attract lonesome women who had more money than brains. Casey's long-suffering mother had understood this and set him free, but had continued to love him until the day she died.

"Hello, Eddie. Do I really look that bad?"

"Worse than I expected," he said frankly. "That fellow Murdock said there was nothing critical about your condition, and that there was no need for me to rush to your bedside. He failed to mention that you look as if you'd been through World War Two."

"Thanks a lot," Casey said dryly.

Eddie turned abruptly as if just realizing someone else was in the room. He smiled at the nurse, showing rows of perfect teeth that he spent a fortune to maintain.

"How about putting these posies in a little water, sweetheart?" He handed the flowers to her and managed to lay a hand on her arm at the same time. Eddie was a toucher. He smiled and he touched and most of the time he completely charmed the females he did it to. The young nurse was no exception. A rosy glow flooded her face as he continued to stare at her as if his eyes couldn't leave her face.

"I'll see if I can find a pretty vase to put them in," she answered shyly as the magic of Eddie Farrow worked again. She smiled sweetly, her eyes clinging to his.

"Hurry back," he said, the words coming from deep in his throat.

Eddie didn't move until the nurse left the room. That was another trick of his to make a woman feel special. When the door closed softly behind her, he eased himself down onto the chair and pulled at the creases in his trousers.

"You never miss an opportunity to practice. You're always improving on your technique," Casey said crossly. Any other time she would have smiled at her father's flirtation.

"Of course, practice makes perfect." Eddie was undaunted by her sarcasm. "To be able to attract the opposite sex is an art, Cassandra. Eye contact is the main thing. I—" He broke off when she waved her hand impatiently, then continued with determination. "I could teach you how to get any man you want, if you'd just listen. Before long—"

"Knock it off, Eddie. We've been down this road

before. I'm in no mood for a lecture on how to snag a rich husband," she said bitterly and drew an unsteady breath that caused a sharp pain in her rib cage.

"I am only trying to help you, Cassandra," he said with just the right catch in his voice to make her regret her sharp words.

He really was quite handsome, Casey reflected sadly. His face was tanned from his Hawaiian vacation with Mrs. Somebody or other, and there was just the right amount of gray sprinkling his dark hair to make him look worldly, mature. All she inherited from him was his height and the color of his eyes. She thanked God she got her scruples from her mother because he had none at all. His next statement verified that.

"If we play our cards right, we can get a good-sized settlement out of this guy, Murdock. I understand he ran into you. The bastard was negligent! Any jury would look at you and tell you're scarred for life. What about your career? You had a good chance to go right to the top in that company, but now—"

"Eddie, stop it! There'll be no lawsuit," Casey said sharply. "It was just as much my fault as his. I was warned to stay off the highway. Visibility was zero. I thought I would take a chance. I was tired and wanted to get home. The man at the station where I got gas warned me that there had already been one bad accident. Besides . . ." she started to say more, but in an instant decided not to reveal the other reason why the accident could have been her fault alone.

"If you were warned to stay off the highway, so was he," Eddie said stubbornly.

"That's true," Casey admitted. "But it still isn't enough reason to sue the man. He could turn around and sue me. Have you thought about that?

He could get a judgment against me and I'd be paying on it for the rest of my life."

"You're not being practical. A man in his position must have tons of insurance."

"What do you mean? Have you been checking up on him? Eddie, I've told you before, don't interfere in my life!" Anger flamed through her body.

"Don't get in a snit, love. You're in no condition to make a quick decision," Eddie said firmly. "Dan Murdock is one of the lumber company Murdocks. I don't know how he fits in, but I'll find out."

"Eddie!" She wanted to shriek at him, but it came out a low, menacing snarl. "I'm perfectly able to take care of my own affairs without any help from you. Need I remind you that I've been doing it for quite some time. And . . . by the way, I'll be needing that five hundred I loaned you last year."

Eddie laughed. "You look just like your mother when you're all steamed up."

"Don't try to get around me by bringing up mother. She was too good for you and you know it," Casey snapped. "I'm not kidding about needing the money. I may be out of a job."

"All the more reason to—"

"No! I've got insurance, which will help, and some savings. Dan Murdock saved my life. I'm not going to repay him by dragging him through the courts."

"It appears to me he's taken an inordinate amount of interest in you, cookie. Maybe you have other plans for him?" he said hopefully.

"You're making me angry," Casey said quietly. "Go away and come back another time. And by the way, what were you doing in Seattle?"

"Business and . . . pleasure. A friend of mine has property up there and she wanted me to look it over."

"Why? You don't have a license to sell real estate in Washington."

"Who said anything about selling?" Eddie answered, his laugh wide, emphasizing the tiny dimples at each corner of his perfectly groomed mustache.

"You're hopeless!" Casey exclaimed, but there was a fondness in her eyes as she looked at him.

"What a thing to say to your father!" He got to his feet with a stricken look on his face as if he took parenting seriously.

"You should have been an actor."

"Should have been? I am an actor. Life is a series of one-act plays and I play a part in each of them." He touched her cheek with one finger. "But I care very much about my only offspring."

"How do you know?"

"How do I know what? That I care—"

"No," she interrupted. "How do you know that I'm your only offspring? Do I have brothers and sisters floating around out there?" She lifted her hand in a circling gesture.

"Who can say?" he said dramatically. "Who knows what seeds we sow as we travel life's highways? I think John Barrymore said that."

"It figures," Casey said dryly. "Bye, Eddie. Thanks for the flowers."

The nurse didn't return to the room for quite some time after Eddie left and Casey assumed he had detained her in the hallway. She dismissed him from her thoughts as the image of Dan Murdock crowded into her mind.

She had seen nothing of him for several days, but he had called her each evening since he was away. He talked freely about himself.

His family had lumber interests near Bend. He was there, now, negotiating with a foreign buyer. Business had been slow due to the building slump and they had been forced to lay off some of the workers. The new contract would mean jobs, he told her, and they were cutting the profit built into their bid to the limit in order to provide those jobs.

He asked if her father had been to see her and if she had heard from her employer. At that time she had answered no to both questions. Last evening she told him she didn't need the private nurse, but he insisted she keep her on for a few more days.

Casey gazed out the window as evening approached and tried to visualize his face. His features appeared vaguely in her mind's eye, but she could clearly see wide shoulders, the strong line of his body, a firm waistline tapering to lithe hips, the chest molded to a soft white shirt, and long muscled legs which moved with assurance. He was physically in the peak of condition. As a male specimen, Casey mused, he was unquestionably superb.

During their phone conversations she was careful to speak to him with the quiet courtesy of a stranger, answering his questions and asking none of her own. Eddie was right about him showing an unusual amount of interest in her. Why? Did he feel guilty? A part of her hoped he never called again, the other part listened for the ring of the phone.

Casey had had her share of emotional entanglements during the last ten years. She had lost her virginity her first year out of high school. It shocked her into the realization that she was following her mother down the primrose path with a handsome rake who had no intentions of being true to her. After that at least three times a year some would-be seducer laid siege to her body, but Casey remained inviolate. And she was determined to make herself financially secure so she would never be forced to do the menial work her mother had done.

But she'd never met a man who'd come even close to being anything like Dan Murdock, she realized suddenly. Bits and pieces of conversation kept coming back to her. Things about reincarnation, and about him knowing she was special to him. She wished her mind had been clear that night and she could have asked him what he was talking about. Suddenly she hoped it would be a long, long time before she saw him again. She didn't need his pity. The thought of him looking at her as if she were a caterpillar crawling out of his salad caused her to close her eyes and clench her teeth. She went cold, then hot as she imagined how she must have looked to him—black ringed eyes, face swollen beneath the bandages, her hands like chicken's feet! And that was the part of her he could see. The doctor told her she had over fifty stitches in her right breast. She had no intention of going bare breasted on a public beach so that part of her injuries had been relegated to the back of her mind, although she was acutely aware that she would never again be able to wear a sleeveless sundress, a low-cut evening dress, or appear on the beach in a skimpy bathing suit.

The door opened and closed softly. Casey kept her face turned toward the window and blinked rapidly at the tears in her eyes. Miss Peachy-Complexion would be going off duty soon. She was sick to death of the girl hovering over her. She opened her mouth to tell her not to turn on the lights when a whiff of something masculine reached her nose. An icy hand squeezed her heart and Dan's deep voice said, "Hello, Casey."

She turned startled eyes toward him and at the same time burrowed her hands and arms beneath the sheet. Her eyes ran over Dan quickly before she turned her head away. The movement was too quick and she flinched from the pain as her ear and cheek pressed into the pillow. He was just as she remembered—a man totally in command of himself. Finally she remembered to return his greeting.

"Hello."

There was silence. "May I sit down?"

"Be my guest," she said ungraciously, keeping her face turned away from him.

"Thanks." He carried the chair around the end of the bed and placed it so that when he sat down his eyes were only a couple of feet from hers.

There was nowhere for Casey to look but at him. He was wearing a brown shirt with pearl snaps and tight-fitting, Western cut slacks of tan corduroy. It wasn't his casual attire that held her attention, but the rugged planes of his tanned features, lean and strong. She had had no difficulty remembering his size or the dark glitter of his eyes, but she had forgotten about the unruliness of his thick, dark hair. She watched the straight, firm line of his mouth curve in a smile that softened the hard contours of his face.

Casey lay stiffly, all her nerve ends tingling under the scrutiny of those eyes. She knew she had never looked as unattractive as she did then. There was no artificial cause for the color that tinged her cheeks as his gaze traveled over her face, taking in the bruises beneath her eyes, the unwashed hair pulled back from her face, and the dressing that covered her cheek and ear leaving the stitches visible across her forehead.

Her gold-flecked eyes held a definite shimmer of defiance when she met his glance. All her defenses were raised. Casey didn't fully understand this inner need to protect herself from him, it was just there and seemed to be purely instinctive. The strong mouth slanted its line, but it never made the full transition into a smile. His glance locked with hers.

"Hello again. Why are you so cross tonight? Did you have a bad day?"

She wanted to say, Hell, yes, I had a bad day. Every day from now on will be a bad day. But it would be a gross display of bad manners.

"I'm sorry. I didn't mean to sound cross." Her throat felt as if it had a rock in it.

He bent forward and she imagined she felt his breath on her face. "We don't need false politeness between us, Casey. If you had a bad day, say, Hell, yes, I had a lousy day."

Oh, God! Can he read my mind? "Hell, yes. I had a lousy day today and expect to have a lousier one tomorrow," she blurted out.

"That's better. It's natural to resent what's happened to you. Don't keep that resentment bottled up inside. It'll be easier if you share it with me."

Her retort was quick. "You don't know anything about it. I've only seen you twice in my life."

"In this life, but not in the others." He made the statement a challenge and his eyes gleamed with amusement as the corners of his mouth lifted.

"I think you're missing a few bricks!"

He threw his head back and laughed. "No, you don't. Haven't you ever felt as if you've done something before, known someone before, looked on something beautiful before? The feeling only lasts for an instant, but it's very real at the time. That's the way I feel about you. We could have rowed the Nile as Mark Anthony and Cleopatra; reveled in Camelot as Sir Lancelot and Queen Guinevere; walked the shores of the Deschutes River as an Indian brave and his maiden; or come across the great plains as man and wife on a wagon train. Think about it. Do I seem like a stranger to you?"

The question caught her off guard. She was conscious of the uneven hammering of her pulse under the steady gaze of his dark eyes. He didn't seem like a stranger, but she wouldn't admit it to him!

"If I knew you in another life, more than likely I was a rabbit and you were a hawk!"

"No. If you were a rabbit I was a rabbit." The dark gray eyes danced with pure mischief. "Our life was short, but we did our share to insure the future of the species."

Casey's stomach churned with a violent emotion, which she interpreted as anger. The frown of disapproval she shot at him did nothing but intensify the devilish grin on his face.

A man this attractive must have someone at home, she thought, even if he wasn't wearing a wedding ring. She had another thought on the heels of that one. With his strength and gentleness, he would be a warm and demanding lover.

She wanted to say something clever to let him know the conversation was getting too personal and that she didn't appreciate his humor. She looked into dark friendly eyes and suddenly the matter was out of her hands. She smiled, a wobbly, halfhearted smile.

"I rather left myself wide open for that one," she said shakily.

"You have a very beautiful mouth, Casey Farrow," he said softly. "I'll see to it that it smiles more often."

Her mood instantly changed back to anger. "Don't practice your moves on me, Sir Lancelot. I don't know what field you think you're playing on, or what you hope to gain by tossing out flowers. I've already told you I'm not going to file a legal claim against you." The anger in her eyes was echoed in her voice.

Dan switched on the lamp on the bedside table, replacing the gloom with soft light. Although he was still lounging in his chair, an electricity emanated from him. Casey knew that she had angered him. She stared into dark eyes and desperately asked herself how things could have developed to such a point. Where was her painfully acquired discipline and self-control?

"We may just as well get this relationship started off on the right foot, Casey." His face had a harshness that made her shiver.

"There's no relationship between us, Mr. Murdock." She felt shaken and a little out of breath, but compelled to retort caustically.

"Oh, but there is!" His voice was soft, but the measured words left no doubt as to their rock-hard meaning. "I'm very attracted to you. I'm thirty-four years old and you are the first woman I've ever wanted in any way other than physically, and that's not saying that I don't want you that way, too. After you get to know me, you'll find that I don't pass out compliments lightly. I meant it when I said you have a beautiful mouth and I also mean it when I say you have a hard, cynical attitude."

"What you're saying is ridiculous! I'm not . . . hard or cynical," she blurted out, and moved her head so suddenly on the pillow that she winced. "You don't know anything about me, and . . . my personal life is none of your business."

"I do know about you. I hadn't planned on having this conversation just yet. I wanted to wait until you were stronger." He paused and raised his brows in question, but Casey was too dumbfounded to speak. He reached over and lifted her hair from her neck and tucked it behind her head. "You have beautiful hair, too. When I was in your apartment I saw the posters of you demonstrating the cosmetic line. I stole one of them."

"You've . . . you've been to my apartment?" Casey's mouth remained agape after she gasped the words.

"Of course. How do you think your personal things got here?" He laughed at the vaguely puzzled look on her face.

"I thought Judy brought them up before she left on one of her flights. She's a stewardess for an international airline and lives next . . ." her voice trailed off in disbelief.

"I met Judy," Dan said matter-of-factly. "She helped select what you'd need. She also told me your rent was due. I paid it for another month, so you needn't worry about that."

"You have a nerve! I've lived there six years. They wouldn't have thrown me out for being a month behind in my rent."

"I realize that under the circumstances your landlord would have waited for the rent money, but it wasn't necessary." He looked at her intently. "Why are your arms covered? Are you cold?"

"No! Yes!" She couldn't think with him sitting so close to her and looking as if he knew every line and hair on her body. Consciously she willed herself to remember that this man was a stranger to her. She knew absolutely nothing about him except what he had told her.

"I like touching you," he said softly, breaking into her thoughts. His hand slid beneath the sheet and his fingers closed around her forearm. "That's better." He smiled into her eyes as if it was the most natural thing in the world for him to caress her arm.

Casey felt the warmth and sense of connection that pulsed so powerfully between them. At the moment it was a quiet, yet profound feeling, but suddenly she was jolted by an instant flash of memory: *This had happened before!* I'm losing my mind was her next thought. Then, overwhelmed by what she was feeling, the stiffness left her body, her eyes lost themselves in the dark, gray depths of his and she seemed to be filled with a warmth and completeness that was new to her. She was conscious of nothing except firm warm fingers on her arm holding her back. But . . . from what?

"I knew you'd relax if I could touch you." His voice came softly through the roar in her ears. "You've been lying there stiff as a board." The hand moved slowly up and down her arm. She had a mad impulse to hug it to her side, to keep the security of his touch with her. "We've got to get you out of here so I can take you home with me."

"What?" Reality returned instantly. "What?" she said again, and her mouth remained open, her lips still forming the word.

Dan laughed, his eyes moving over her face. Firm fingers pressed beneath her chin to push her lips together.

"I want to take you to my home near Bend as soon as you're released from the hospital. You'll be in no condition either physically or mentally to stay alone. We have a big house. You won't have to see anyone if you don't want to, yet we're only fifteen minutes from town. You'll love the—"

"Hold it! We're not living in the Dark Ages, Sir Lancelot. This is the twentieth century. When I leave this hospital I'm going straight back to my apartment and try to get my life back together. I've got six months to wait before the plastic surgeon can work on my . . . face. I still need to find out if my insurance will cover the cost of that and if I have a job." She paused. The little short breaths she was forced to take because of her hurt ribs were not enough to allow for a long speech. Dan didn't take advantage of the pause to speak. He waited patiently, his rough fingertips finding the pulsing vein in her wrist and holding it.

"Don't plan my life," she sputtered. "Not one day, one week, or one month. I won't stand for it!"

She wondered if he knew her stomach was like a washing machine. Irritated at the thought that he knew so much about her, she said, "Leave me alone, Mr. Murdock, I'm a big girl. I can take care of myself!" She stared at him with a defiant look.

The quiet hung heavily after her outburst. He smiled and her blood ran cold. She stared at him in almost total panic, because in that smile had been threat, amusement, implacable determination, and admiration. The realization that he was being as tolerant of her outburst as if she were a stubborn child frightened her. She had the inescapable feeling that she could run from him all she liked, but he would be behind her every step of the way.

"I admire your independence," he said softly. "I realize you and your mother had it pretty rough after your father left you. But don't let what he did cloud your opinion of me. I won't disappoint you. I'm delighted to find my Guinevere still somewhat inexperienced and man-wary at age twenty-seven. You have a freshness about you, an inner beauty that I'm attracted to." His smile held a hint of possessiveness.

"I'm not attracted to you at all," Casey lied, struggling to rally her defenses against him, but it was like swimming upstream against a strong current.

"You didn't mind my kiss the other night. I'd really like to kiss you again if you promise not to snap at me." The glitter in his eyes made her feel as though her heart might leap from her breast. She was too stunned to answer and her lips parted softly in surprise. "I think I'll take my chances," he said, lowering his mouth to hers.

At first the kiss was gentle as he explored without haste the flavor and texture of her mouth. His tongue stroked her lips, sweetly, hesitantly, but did not enter her mouth as if waiting for an invitation before the first tender invasion. Never had she been kissed like this before. Her mind fed on the new sensations created by his firm but gentle lips, the feel of his teeth, his tongue, the freshness of his mouth, and even the hardness of his nose lying beside hers.

He made the world spin.

When she did not protest—when in fact she welcomed it—he deepened the kiss with a mounting urgency. A wild crescendo rose within her and she felt she had become one with Dan and then an extension of him. That was how it would be if he made love to her, she realized. She wanted to fill her arms with his rock-hard body, nuzzle the cheeks that needed to be shaved twice a day. She longed to surround and enfold him in an intimate embrace.

His lips softened, caressed, and clung with a leisurely sweetness that held still the very moments of time. He lifted his head; his half-shuttered eyes looked into hers and her gaze wavered beneath his direct stare. A deep, inner restlessness flickered to life in the pit of her stomach.

"You see how it is? We can't control our destiny, my Guinevere." His lips briefly touched her nose. "And don't be difficult about this, sweetheart. Go with the tide." He stood abruptly. "Don't say anything," he cautioned. "Don't say anything at all." And with a faint brushing of his mouth against hers, he was gone.

Casey stared at the closed door. Damned if I'm not beginning to believe him, she thought.

Three

"And you'll have a five-year supply of Allure products," Neil Hamilton said as if he were giving her the earth. He moved restlessly about the room, edging ever closer to the door. "If something opens up in the office, later on, we'll give you a call. Meanwhile, you'll have your workman's compensation. God knows I've paid enough into that fund." His voice had an irritated twang to it.

Thanks for nothing, Neil, Casey thought bitterly. I know, and you know, that you wouldn't have a face like mine in your office. Every woman who worked for him was a walking advertisement for Allure. There was murder in Casey's amber eyes as she looked at him. Damn him, she'd like to see what he would do in her position. How would he handle it? The bastard! He couldn't even look at her!

"Jennifer will be able to take over your territory. God, I was lucky to get her." He paused and glanced at Casey. "I'll send her up to see you so you can give her a few pointers."

Casey met his cool gaze and struggled back from the edge of that yawning pit of rage and misery that stretched before her. Summoning all the discipline, both mental and physical, for which she had fought so hard during the years she had been on her own, she refused to give way before this machine of a man.

"Don't count on me to help her, Neil. I'm leaving Portland," she said steadily.

"Surely you won't be leaving for a few days."

"Probably not for a few weeks," she told him bitterly and let what she didn't say speak for her.

With his smooth brows raised, Neil moved to the side of the bed and looked down at her. Casey would have had to be blind not to see the annoyed frown flash across his carefully composed features, or the scathing look in his eyes.

"You're refusing to help after all I've done for you?"

"Yes. Just as you're refusing to help me because I've been unfortunate enough to be disfigured in an accident. Let your Jennifer Carwilde learn the ropes the hard way, like I did." Her voice rose in spite of her determination to stay calm. Angry resentment churned inside her, screaming to be released. "I gave you sixteen hours of my time every day for seven years, Neil. I've got seven years of experience and a scarred face. What has Jennifer Carwilde got?" she hissed, her angry eyes locking with his.

"She's got a natural beauty that makes every woman who sees her green with envy and crazy to look just like her," he said with cold deliberation. "I'll pay you for the time you spend with her. She's smart. She'll learn fast."

"You don't have that much money, Neil."

"You'd better knock off the sarcasm, Casey.

You're forgetting who you're talking to. You're going to need references if you work again."

"Don't threaten me, you egotist! You don't have the brains of a flea! That business will go down the drain within the next five years because you haven't the foresight to deal with today's market and you can't see anything beyond a pretty face and a firm little behind. Now get the hell out of here!"

Casey could see him tense as if he were coiling to retaliate with physical force, but his words struck her more cruelly than the back of his hand against her face might have.

"And what are you, Casey Farrow, but a scarred broad? No amount of makeup will help and you'll never work in the cosmetic field again!"

"Maybe not. But I've got it together on the inside where it counts," she flung back desperately. "Now get out!" She fairly screamed the words, her control almost gone. "You sorry excuse for a human being! Get out! Get out!" Pushing herself up on her elbow, she bit back a groan at the pounding ache in her head. The man before her, the table beside the bed, the white-walled room, all wove in and out of the red shadows threatening to engulf her. Her head throbbed, sending waves of nausea through her and she lay back.

"You'll be sorry for this." The voice came through a soft fuzziness that muffled even the sound of the door being flung open.

"What the hell . . .? Who are you?" Dan demanded as two strides brought him to the side of the bed. A muscle twitched alongside his mouth and he clenched and unclenched his fists, as if it cost him great effort not to use them.

"I'm her *ex-boss*, if it's any of your business. The last boss she'll ever have in the cosmetic industry!"

Hard hands grasped Neil by the shoulders and

spun him around. "Mister, you don't know how close you are to losing some teeth." There was murder in the dark eyes and Neil recognized it.

For several seconds, Casey was sure she was going to faint. Panic gripped her. Dan, Neil . . . fighting? Neil was trying to shrug off the hands holding him, and Dan was propelling him to the door with the force of a hurricane.

"Get your hands off me! You haven't heard the last of this!" Neil's voice had lost its arrogant tone and was almost a whine.

"Listen, because I'm saying this only once. I'll be at your office in one hour to collect her wages. Have checks ready for back pay plus a month's vacation. You're damned lucky I don't break both your legs. Now, get!" A thrust of the powerful arms sent Neil into the hall.

Casey didn't hear the door close or the footsteps bringing the big man to her bedside. She lay with her eyes closed. Beneath the covering her hands gripped each other, as the pain of Neil's words jabbed at her again and again. *Scarred . . . Scarred . . . Scarred . . .* She wanted nothing more than to slip into comforting oblivion and let sweet numbness drift over her. She'd had a taste of life's cruelties before, but nothing had ever demoralized her like this. In a few short moments he had stripped her of will, physical courage, even the ability to reason. Something deep and primitive screamed from her very center that it wasn't fair that this should happen to her. The tears began to flow. They came in a torrent from the depths of her misery. She tried to turn on her side, away from the door. The sheet slipped down over her shoulder, but even in her near hysterical state, she was conscious of it and frantically bunched it up about her neck.

Harsh sobs tore from her throat, bringing acute pain to her tortured body as her stomach and chest convulsed. She could no more stop them than she could a rumbling freight train. For the first time in her life she was totally beaten, totally without spirit.

"Casey . . . don't cry." Dan sat on the edge of the bed. "The loss of a job isn't the end of the world. Shhh . . . don't cry." His voice was pleading, but she wouldn't be comforted. The shame and humiliation she had felt during the confrontation with Neil came surging back, and she resisted the hand on her shoulder, trying to shrug it away in spite of the pain that knifed through her injured breast.

"Go away," she sobbed. "Go! Don't look at me!" She pulled the sheet up over her face.

"All right. I won't look at you if you don't want me to. But don't cry. That bastard isn't worth one tear from your eyes."

"You . . . don't understand. Please go." The agonized voice came from beneath the sheet.

"I can't leave you like this, Casey." Then he uttered a searing epithet which revealed his anger. "I could break that bastard's neck," he swore. His hand burrowed beneath the covering and his fingers caressed the soft skin on her inner forearm. "Don't worry about losing that lousy job. Things will work out, I promise they will."

"I don't care about the job." Her soft voice quavered and even more tears squeezed out from under the tightly closed lids. "I don't care about the . . . damned job," she repeated.

"Then what is it? Shhh . . . you'll make yourself sick crying like this." His voice lowered to a husky whisper. "Let me help you, Casey." The sympathy in his voice jarred against her already taut nerves.

"Don't feel sorry for me!" she lashed out. "I don't need you . . . or anyone." She tried to jerk her arm from his grasp, but his fingers tightened.

"You don't need me to feel sorry for you. You're doing a good job of it yourself." She could hear the words, but they weren't making sense. "Was he your lover? Is that why you're wallowing in all this self-pity?"

Damn him! She jerked the sheet away from her face. "No! I wouldn't have slept with that slimy little toad if he was the last man on earth!" Anger crowded out the hurt.

"Good. I didn't think he was your type."

"Well, you're not my type either, Sir Lancelot, so you might just as well get on your trusty steed and gallop off into the sunset," she replied shrewishly.

"I've got to polish my armor first."

She clamped her mouth shut and wished desperately that she was anywhere in the world but here, lying helplessly in bed with Dan's hand clamped to her arm. Damn! Damn him!

He read her thoughts and lifted his brows in a way that made her want to strike out at him. "You're going to have to learn, my Guinevere, that disappointment and grief are made easier if shared with someone who cares about you. Now tell your knight what's troubling you, other than the fact that you've lost your job."

"If you're thinking you'll go forth and do battle for me, Lancelot, forget it. I can fight my own battles."

"I don't doubt that one bit, Guinevere. But it would be much easier for you if I fought beside you."

Her eyes burned up at him resentfully. "I'm not your damned Guinevere. I don't intend to end up in a convent on some isolated coast. So forget it!"

"And I don't intend to end up in a monastery like Lancelot. But that's beside the point." His dark eyes were teasing and a secretive smile curved his mouth. Bending forward, he brushed his lips tantalizingly across hers.

"Stop that!"

He laughed. "Things didn't turn out so great for Lancelot and Guinevere, but that doesn't mean they won't for us."

With a groan of irritation, she turned away from him. "I wish you'd never come here!"

"No, you don't. Besides, I had nothing to do with it." Amusement glinted in his dark eyes. "It just happened. It was destined to happen."

She rolled her head to look at him. He was grinning broadly. Her eyes challenged him and her thoughts whirled.

"Don't give me any more of that reincarnation gibberish. I don't buy it. But . . . if I did have another life I was probably Cleopatra and you were the asp that bit me!" The words exploded from her tense lips and her eyes flashed at him.

He laughed aloud. "And I enjoyed biting your soft bosom."

"I'm glad you're amused," she snapped. There was mischief in his dark eyes. Without thinking, she allowed the edges of her lips to curl upward. "You've got to be the most exasperating man I've ever met."

"Thank you," he said with mock politeness. "At least I've got your attention." He plucked a tissue from the box on the table and wiped her eyes. "Okay. We've crossed this hurdle, let's go on to the next."

"What hurdle?"

"Shhh . . . and listen. I'll go to your office and pick up your checks. Do you have any personal things you want me to bring back?"

"You don't need to do this." She couldn't quite revive the sting in her voice that she had before. "I can get Judy to pick up my things."

"Do you?" he insisted.

"Yes," she said tiredly. "Linda McNiece, the office manager, will clean out my desk."

Dan picked up the phone from the bedside table. "What's the number?" Casey gave it to him and he dialed. "Linda McNiece, please. Hello, Linda. This is Dan Murdock, Casey Farrow's fiancé." He clamped his hand over the mouthpiece when a gasp of protest escaped Casey's lips. "You didn't know she was engaged? I'm surprised she didn't tell you. Oh, yes, we've known each other for years." Several hundred, he mouthed to Casey, and her lips tightened angrily. "Yes, we think it's a good time for her to leave the company. We're planning a family as soon as she's able. We both love kids." We didn't get a chance to have any before, he mouthed silently and Casey fumed. "I'll be down shortly, Linda. I'd appreciate it if you'd pack up Casey's belongings and I'll pick them up along with her checks." He winked at Casey and she looked defiantly into his twinkling eyes. "Thank you. Yes, she's doing fine now that I'm here to take care of her. See you in a while." He hung up the phone.

"You . . . had no right to tell her that!" Casey sputtered. "We're not engaged! I hardly know you."

"She doesn't know that, Cleo."

"But I know it, you . . . you asp!"

Laugh lines fanned out from his eyes and they sparkled at her through thick lashes. His hand found hers beneath the covering and he took it gently in his. "Am I going to have to bite you again?"

"Oh, Dan! Don't do this to me." She pressed her lips tightly to keep from smiling. "Can't you see, I don't want to laugh. I want to be mean and bitchy. I feel awful and I want everyone else to feel awful, too. Just go away and let me feel sorry for myself."

"You can be as bitchy as you want next week, but not today or tomorrow."

"Why next week?"

"Because I won't be here. I'm going to Japan for

about ten days. Get all the bitchiness out of you while I'm gone." He bent closer. Under slanting black brows his eyes were clear and searching. There was a long, breathless silence. "Will you miss me?" It was scarcely more than a whisper.

Strange tempestuous feelings threatened to swamp her. She was panting a little and drew the tip of her tongue across dry lips while her eyes focused on the sensual fullness of his mouth. Her brain commanded her to tell him that she would be pleased to see the last of him, but her tongue ignored the order. Her eyes closed as if to blot out the problem, then sprang open as she felt the gentle touch of his lips against her cheek. Writhing in the trap he made by leaning over her, she uttered a faint cry of protest.

"Shhh . . . hh. Shhh . . ." His voice was soothing. His lips moved against her unscarred cheek while she struggled desperately to keep her wits about her.

"Do I overwhelm you? Am I going too fast?" His voice was thick. "I don't play games, Casey. When I find something I want, I go for it."

The bold possessiveness of his words, the sheer arrogance of them, sent a thrill of excitement through her even while her intelligence rebelled against them. She made a last attempt to assert control over her mind, only to find that her senses were being led into open rebellion by the touch of his lips as they traveled up to her eyelids and then down to her lips, pressed softly, nibbled, and caressed and possessed. He raised his head and looked searchingly into her eyes.

"This break will give you time to get used to me. I won't rush you into anything, but when I get back we've got some decisions to make."

Confusion darkened Casey's eyes while her bewildered mind groped for an answer. She rolled her head on the pillow helplessly, and her lips formed the word no, but it didn't come out of her mouth.

He watched the expressions flit across her face. "I'm going to talk with the doctor now, then pick up your things and take them to your apartment. What shall I do with the checks? I'll deposit them if you give me a deposit slip from your checkbook."

When he left her, he walked with quick sure steps to the door, turned and threw her a smile over his shoulder before disappearing into the hall.

Casey lay quietly for a long while mulling over his words. *When I find something I want, I go for it. . . .* She couldn't get the words out of her mind. She realized she had never been more vulnerable. She was physically and emotionally wrung out. Was that why she was allowing this man to take over her affairs so completely? The next time she saw him, she promised herself, she would thank him for all he had done for her, then tell him to leave her alone. Oh, dear Lord, she thought, I don't need this!

Dan left for Japan on Monday. He came by for a brief visit Sunday night, and Casey tried to explain her feelings.

"I'll be out of here by the time you return. Thanks for everything. You've been a great help. I don't want you to think I don't appreciate it, but I can go it alone. I always have." She was sitting in a chair beside the bed. It was the first time she had looked at him from an upright position. Somehow he looked larger, more sure of himself than ever.

"I knew you'd look like that in the blue robe," he said, ignoring her carefully rehearsed speech. "When I get back we'll talk to the doctor and set up some kind of timetable for checkups, then we'll go to Bend. You'll love it there."

"Dan! Hold it! I'm getting damned tired of you making plans for me. I've told you this repeatedly and I know you're not dense!"

"No, Casey, I'm not dense, just determined. My mother has a house in Bend that needs someone in it. She travels a lot and has difficulty finding a reliable house-sitter. The job will be perfect for you." He sat on the edge of the bed. She was acutely aware of his broad chest and lean, muscular body. He radiated more masculinity than any man she had ever met.

"Are you still on a guilt trip?" she asked sharply because she had to say something to cover the feeling that she was being taken over.

His hand reached out and grabbed her forearm and jerked her hand out of her pocket. "Why do you always hide your hands?" He spread her fingers out on his palm and rubbed a forefinger gently over the healing ridges on the back of her hand.

"You're not blind. You can see why!" She glared at him and tried to pull her hand away, but he tucked an uninjured finger between his and refused to release it.

"Is a beautiful exterior so important to you?"

"You think I'm a vain, silly woman, don't you? Let me tell you, Mr. Dan Murdock, a woman has to use any means available in order to survive. For seven years I made my living with these hands. I've cared for them as if they were a piece of expensive equipment. Now, look at them. How would they look holding a jar of skin lotion or a bottle of glossy nail enamel?"

"I hadn't thought about it like that."

The concern in his voice and the unhappy look on his face were almost her undoing. She choked back the lump that rose in her throat and looked away from him. *Dammit, why did he have to be so understanding?* He barged into her life and had been more concerned for her, given her more help and understanding, than anyone since her mother died. Casey didn't know how to handle it so she hid behind flippancy.

"At least I can wipe my own nose while I'm crying about it." She tried to smile, but her lips felt like rubber. She tried to keep her voice light, but it rasped harshly.

"Are you still taking the pain pills?"

"No. I don't take any more medication than necessary. I don't believe in it."

"Good girl! My sentiments exactly." He got to his feet slowly and loomed over her. She didn't attempt to tilt her head up to look at him. "Think about what I said about house-sitting for my mother. When I get back we'll talk about it some more."

"I can tell you right now—no! I'm not destitute. I've no need for Murdock welfare. Thanks, but no thanks," she said with firm determination.

He sat back down on the bed. "There are times when I would get great satisfaction from turning you across my knee and smacking your backside. Pride is great but you're carrying it in front of you like a shield. Put it down, Casey. There's no room for pride between you and me." His battered features took on a no-nonsense look and the thought passed through her mind that he would make a relentless enemy. He had powerful shoulders and arms. She wondered if at one time he had worked as a lumberjack.

His dark eyes roamed her face. She had known he was coming, but had made no attempt to beautify herself other than brush her hair. She had cut it a little shorter around her face, so that it fell forward over her bandaged ear and swirled low over her forehead to partially hide the deep red-puckered flesh.

"I'm sure your head is still in the Dark Ages, Lancelot, where women were beaten into submission when they refused to walk behind their *lords*. This is the twentieth century and I may be a *damsel in distress*, but I need no further help. There's no reason for you to feel responsible for me. There's no reason for us to quarrel. We're strangers to each other and I think it's better to keep it that way."

The hard-edged line of his jaw and the sudden narrowing of his eyes warned her that he was angry and stopped her from saying anything else. She turned her head deliberately, giving him a view of her profile.

"That's not true, Casey, and you know it, but I won't argue the point now." His voice rasped across her nerve ends like chalk on a blackboard. She couldn't help the wave of apprehension that caused a shiver to travel the length of her spine. Strange, she thought, how the same voice could be so comforting one moment and so grating in its harshness the next. This was a very complex man.

His voice was dangerously soft, now. "I want to leave with a better feeling between us, but I can see you're not going to let me do that."

"So you're finally getting the drift." The silence that followed made her more ashamed of those words than any she had uttered in a long while. She had to apologize. It went against her nature to be rude and especially to this man regardless of how he worried her. "I'm sorry, Dan." She turned tear-filled eyes in his direction, hating herself for not being able to hold them back. "Please . . . I'm trying hard to cope with this change in my life. It's difficult for me to handle anything else." She was proud of her level voice. It in no way matched the erratic beat of her heart.

Warm fingertips caressed the side of her face and moved around her ear while dark eyes studied her.

"I understand how you feel, but it'll be easier if

you stop fighting me . . . and yourself. We won't say any more about a relationship between us. I'll be back a week from Wednesday to check you out of here." Casey leaned her head against the back of the chair so she could look up at him. "Stand up, Casey," he said half under his breath with his eyes intent on her flushed face. "I'd like to see you standing before I go."

Casey found herself obeying mechanically. She felt weak in the knees, but stood with her eyes fastened on his face. She could feel the warmth of his body, far too close to hers, and the warmth of the telltale blood that rushed into her face. To hide it, she bent her head, and looked down at the hand that held hers. Firm fingers beneath her chin tilted her head upward and her eyes locked with his and drew all coherent thinking from her mind.

"I wanted to see you standing beside me," he said softly. "What I really want to do is hold you in my arms, but I'm afraid I'll hurt you." She studied his face. It told her nothing except that he was fascinated by her expression. "Why are you surprised?"

Casey opened her mouth, but no sound came out. She moistened her dry lips. She felt as if she were in a vacuum, being drawn toward him.

"You're . . . taller than I thought you were," she said.

"So are you. And I'm glad. I won't have to bend so far to kiss you." The words were so softly spoken they barely reached her ears. Strange sensations went zigzag along her nerve endings. She wanted to say something flip and clever, but his hands were on her back—almost the only place on her body spared the laceration of the flying glass— and the sensuous dance of his fingertips made rational thought impossible.

"You're a fraud, my Guinevere. On the surface you appear to be a typical example of an extremely

liberated woman, but underneath you're soft, vulnerable, and would like very much to have someone to lean on, to share life's joys and sorrows
with. I intend to be that man and you might as
well accept it." He smiled, the firm lips flattened
against even white teeth. The smile was wicked,
teasing, and jarred her to her senses.

"Why do you always have to say something that
makes me angry!" She hoped desperately that he
didn't know how nervous and excited she was.

He chuckled softly, his face alive with amusement.

"Somehow I can't resist. You respond to teasing
so beautifully." His hand was beneath the hair at
the back of her neck and he applied a small amount
of pressure. "Lay your head on my shoulder for
just a moment and see how comforting it is. I
won't hold you tightly, though I want to." His
soft voice droned on with those unreal words and
she found herself obeying. "Is this your injured
breast?" Gentle fingertips on her bandaged breast
accompanied the question.

"Yes," she murmured quietly.

They stood for a long moment, her smooth cheek
resting against his shoulder, his large hands moving gently over her back. Casey closed her eyes
and let her other senses take over. She felt the
soft texture of his shirt, heard the thump of his
heartbeat, smelled the now familiar mint smell of
his breath. It was pleasant, comforting to be em-
braced by strong arms, sheltered . . . cherished.

Her eyes flew open. What was the matter with
her? What was she doing? She couldn't let herself
depend on this man, or any man!

"No. No . . ." he said softly as he felt her with-
drawal. "Stay here and kiss me good-bye. You're
like a bird fluttering its wings. C'mon, kiss me.
You'll have ten days to think about whether you
liked it or not."

Without thinking, she closed her eyes, lifted her

face, and offered her lips. His lips pressed upon hers gently, tenderly, and Casey's gave quick answer, returning warm, fleeting kisses. A warm tide of contentment came over her as she realized there was no urgency in his kiss. Her mouth trembled under his.

"No maid of my dreams could taste so sweet, my Guinevere," he breathed against her lips.

The eyes that looked into hers grew radiant, sending her senses reeling, and then there was again the soft union of lips and tongues as their mouths parted. They clung to each other with a leisurely sweetness unaware of the passing time. Then he moved away from her.

"Take care of yourself while I'm gone."

"You, too," she murmured shyly.

He smiled and placed a whisper of a kiss on her lips before he turned sharply and left the room.

Casey looked at the closed door and wondered what strange madness possessed her when she was with Dan. More than likely, she thought, that was the last she'd ever see of Mr. Dan Murdock. Kissing him had been a delightful interlude, but now it was over. She could set her mind to more important matters.

She took off her robe and climbed into bed, but somehow her mind refused to take up the more important matters, and continued to dwell on a tall, dark-haired man.

Four

"You're sure you'll be all right?"

Casey grinned at her friend Judy. "No. I'm going to pop all my stitches and you'll have to call the paramedics."

"My wiseacre friend's back." Judy sighed and handed Casey a frosty glass wrapped in a paper napkin. "Drink this daiquiri and tell me why you got the wild notion to come home."

"I didn't think I could stand that place another day, another hour." Casey lounged on her comfortable recliner and looked around her apartment. "Thanks for watering my plants, they look great."

"Sure." Judy curled up on the end of the couch. She had eight days off, a break in her schedule with the airline that occurred every few months. "Okay. Bring me up to date on everything. And by the way you look great, considering what you've been through."

Casey cast her a wary look. They had been friends for too long for there to be any pretense between them. "Since when did death warmed over look great?"

"No need to say you were damned lucky. You know it."

Judy was a small blonde girl with an infectious grin and boundless energy. She was not exactly beautiful, but pretty. Casey had taught her to do the best with what she had—large brown eyes and a flawless complexion.

"I'm lucky to be alive, but everything else in my life has fallen apart." She closed her eyes briefly, then looked straight at Judy. "You sure find out just how indispensable you are when something like this happens. I still can't believe Neil would fire me after so many years with the company."

"Neil Hamilton's a creepy son of a bitch! You'd already been with the company several years when he came on the scene. He's jealous of your ability and when you rejected his advances that was the last straw. He was waiting for the opportunity to ease you out."

"The hardest part of it is that he's right. I can't demonstrate any more."

Judy looked appalled. "Not now, but how about later? Good heavens! Thousands of women have blemishes on their faces and hands. If you could show them how to look good, despite an imperfection, they'd knock each other down to reach the counter and buy Allure."

"Sounds nice, but Neil won't buy it."

"Allure isn't the only cosmetic firm in the world," Judy said heatedly. "There's a Japanese company trying to gain a foothold in the States. I've met their representative and I know I can get you an interview."

Casey's hand involuntarily crept up to her cheek and nerves knotted in her stomach as she imagined the interviews she would have to go through to get a job. Would she be able to bear the curious stares, the nosy questions? Would the old confidence in her abilities ever return?

"Maybe later, but not now. Just the thought of interviews makes me cringe. I need to get my act together and decide what I'm going to do to support myself. My insurance will cover the plastic surgery, and Dan's taken care of the hospital bill. I've got some savings and Eddie came through with the five hundred he owed me, but I need something to do."

"Okay. I can understand that. What do you want to do? There are other facets to the cosmetic industry besides demonstrating."

"I want nothing more to do with the cosmetic industry," Casey said flatly.

"But . . . look what you're throwing away! All that know-how, all that experience!"

"You can't throw away experience. I'm just walking out on it. I may use it again someday, but not now. Definitely not now."

Judy emptied her glass and unfolded her legs from the couch. "Need another?"

"Sure. Why not? I may sit here and get soused."

"That'll be the day."

Casey closed her eyes while Judy prepared the drinks. The sudden decision to leave the hospital, the argument with Dr. Masters, who reminded her time and again that Dan Murdock wanted her to stay until he returned, the packing, the call to Judy, and the ride home, had tired her more than she expected.

Casey opened her eyes to see Judy standing in front of her with a glass in her hand.

"I had to get out from under the influence of that man or I'd be jumping through a hoop before long," she blurted out.

"You're talking about Dan Murdock, I presume. I'd jump through his hoop any day!" Judy curled up on the couch again and looked steadily at her friend.

Why did I open that can of worms, Casey wondered. It must be the drink. Aloud she said, "Who else?"

"Why don't you like him? I thought he was Tom Selleck and Burt Reynolds rolled into one."

"He isn't my type. I don't like domineering men."

"That's nuts! If I ever find a man who'll wrap me in silk, tuck me into his limousine, and carry me away, he can be just as domineering as he wants to be."

Casey laughed. "You've had plenty of that type. How about the Greek who delayed his trip to New York to camp out on your doorstep?"

"He was fat! He could have tucked me under his number two chin." Judy grimaced and Casey laughed again. "This guy's gone on you, Casey," she said seriously. "He asked me a million questions."

"And I suppose you spilled all."

"My dear, if he'd been a Russian spy I'd have told him how to make the hydrogen bomb."

"Fine friend you turn out to be."

"Don't blame me. Blame that six foot four hunk of masculinity. Why don't I get someone like him on one of my flights?" There was infinite longing in her voice. "I know his family's in the lumber business, but I don't think that's what gave him that . . . that rugged look. Of course, a tree could have fallen on him and pushed his nose to the side, but when I saw the picture in the sports magazine it all made sense." Her bright eyes darted to Casey. "Well, anyway . . . that's that. The mystery is solved. I suppose he told you all about it. Why didn't you say something?" Judy tried to look innocent.

"Would you condescend to tell me what you're talking about?" Casey asked with mock dignity. She knew her friend was teasing, dying to drop her bomb of information. That was one thing Casey loved about their relationship, the light-hearted way they discussed things that were important.

"Well . . . I knew you'd mention it if he'd told you, though I'm surprised he didn't. So, when I turned the page and saw his picture and the head-line: CANADA SALUTES ITS FAVORITE RUGBY PLAYER, I almost jumped up and shouted to everyone in the plane—Hey, I've met him and he's gorgeous!"

"Rugby, eh?" Casey said calmly. "I thought you were going to say a senator or something."

"Senator? Who would get excited over a stuffy old senator?"

"A governor that wants to be one."

"Well, aren't you surprised?" Judy looked disap-pointed.

"Not really," Casey said slowly. No, Sir Lancelot would be right at home on the field of battle, be it a rugby field or a jousting tournament.

"I wonder why he didn't tell you? Or me? We had a long, delicious visit while we packed your things."

"I just bet you did," Casey said. "By the way, will you drive me around tomorrow to look for a good used car? Mine's totaled and the insurance company sent a check, but it's not enough to buy a new one."

"Sure. Maybe we can find one a little old lady used to drive to church on Sunday."

Judy finished her drink and set the glass on the coffee table. "By the way, I've got a special date tomorrow night," she said, her brown eyes alive with excitement. "He's terribly handsome—tall, black hair, mustache, and beautiful blue eyes. He was transferred here from Jacksonville and has the sexiest Southern accent. I'll bring him over for a drink before we go."

"I hope you've checked this one out. He isn't married, is he?"

"Yes, mother, I've checked him out." Lids drooped over brown eyes demurely. "And, no, he isn't married. I met him through another flight attendant whose boyfriend works for the same company. Besides, he doesn't wear a ring," she added in a droll voice.

"Oh, that's a sure sign," Casey said sarcastically, before relenting and letting the obviously excited Judy off the hook. "Do you know anyone who'd want to rent my apartment for a few months?"

"What? You want to sublet? What are you going to do, for Pete's sake?"

"I don't know, but whatever it is, it won't be in Portland. I'm thinking of going to Salem or Corvallis. Either one of those places would be close enough for me to drive back to see the doctor. I can't afford to pay rent on this place and another one, too. Yet, I'll need it later on. The simplest solution would be to sublet for six months."

"When do you want to leave?"

"As soon as possible. Saturday, if I can find a car."

"You won't feel like driving any distance by Saturday," Judy protested. "You're weak as a kitten. What's the big rush to get out of town?"

"I don't want to see anyone. Not Linda, or any of the people I worked with. I especially don't want to see any of that group I went to the beach with this summer. I don't think I could take their sly glances or patronizing attitudes. I just want to be by myself for awhile."

Judy looked sobered. "Okay, okay. Dammit, I think I know how you feel. But let me drive you to wherever you want to go, help you find a room or an apartment, and get you settled in. Then I can take a bus or fly back. You don't have to go right out and find a job, do you? Can't you take a few weeks to get yourself together?"

"I could if I didn't have to worry about this place."

"Leave that to me. Maybe I can rent it to Glen. Ah . . ." She rubbed her hands together and licked her lips. "Wouldn't that be cozy?"

"Glen, the heartthrob from Jacksonville?" Casey knew her friend had seen the quick spurt of tears that filled her eyes, and, knowing sympathy wasn't what she needed, had ignored them.

"No less," Judy said perkily. "Isn't that good thinking on my part?"

"Excellent, if you can swing it."

"I'll give it my best girl scout try." She stood, pulled up her T-shirt and zipped up the fly on her faded jeans. She grinned sheepishly. "It's more comfortable to let it all hang out. Every time I put these things in the dryer they shrink."

"Yeah? Those jeans are at least five years old. C'mon, admit all those late night snacks are getting to you."

"I'm saving my money for the 'fat farm.' That would be the height of luxury—eat all you want and go to a luxurious place where they pamper you and massage off those extra pounds."

"How much do you have to lose? Five pounds? Let's see . . . that would be about five hundred dollars a pound. Pretty expensive for a flight attendant."

"Oh, hush. You're too practical for your own good. I'm going to scoot so you can get some rest. We have a big day tomorrow. I put some of that health food you like in the fridge in case you want a snack." At the door she turned. "I've missed you."

"I've missed you, too. Thanks for everything." Casey's voice was husky with feeling.

Judy always avoided showing any serious emotion if she could possibly help it. "Ah . . . t'was nothing." She waved her hand carelessly. "I rescue damsels in distress every day. Bye. See you in the morning."

She could have talked all day without saying that, Casey thought bitterly. *Damsels in distress.* Three weeks ago the words would have meant nothing. Now, they brought the rugged features of Dan Murdock flashing before her eyes. From now on would everything having to do with knights, kings, and castles make her think of Dan?

After Dan left for Japan it had taken Casey two days to get her thoughts in order and face the fact that any relationship with him was out of the question. She didn't want to be attracted to him and despised that strange tiny butterfly that soared happily through her when he kissed her. There was no way he could possibly be attracted to her in her present condition and whatever game he was playing she wanted no part of it. He was probably the martyr type and had convinced himself that he was responsible for the accident and was determined to atone. Nothing could persuade her to house-sit for his mother! *House-sit!* Another salve for his conscience!

In the quiet of her apartment, Casey squeezed her eyes shut and deliberately brought into her mind the image of her reflection in the mirror that first morning when she viewed her naked body. The breast that had been badly cut by the flying glass was two-thirds the size of the other. A patchwork of puckered scars ranging in color from deep red to dark purple was spread across her stomach, thighs, shoulders, and upper arms. She had held her hair back from her face and absorbed the entire picture of the deep, ugly wound across her forehead to her cheek, ear, and down the length of her body.

For the tiniest moment Casey imagined she was

seeing a body that wasn't her own, then she whimpered softly, grieving for the sleek, slim, flawless body of a month ago. She hadn't appreciated it, taking the satin smooth flesh of her face, shoulders, and arms for granted. Her wardrobe was full of low necked, sleeveless dresses and blouses that she would never wear again. The sight of her naked body had shocked her into realizing she would not, could not, have a physical relationship with any man. The thought of a man viewing her naked body brought the bile to her throat even now, days after the thought had first occurred to her.

The ringing of the phone jarred her from her painful reflections.

"Casey, this is Linda. I called the hospital and they said you were home. I was going to dash up to see you this evening and bring you up to date on the company news. I also want to hear all about your new man. Holy Moses! Where did you find him? I hear he's not only in the chips, no pun intended, but he's a well-known Canadian rugby player."

"You heard right. Say, did Bobby get settled in at his new school?"

"Yes, my one and only offspring is now a military cadet and this house is like a tomb. I thought I might come by this evening if you feel up to having someone around."

"Thanks for thinking about me, Linda, but . . . I . . . I believe my father will be around and, besides, I feel like I've been run over by a steamroller. Can we make it another time?"

"Sure. I want you to know, though, that the rest of the girls and I feel you were given the shaft by our esteemed boss. I'm terribly sorry, Casey. If jobs weren't so hard to find, I'd tell that puffed up pip-squeak where to put mine."

"Thanks. It's probably for the best. It'll force me

to get out and try something new. I feel as though I've had blinders on and seen nothing but my job for the past few years."

"Well, like Dan said you would have quit anyway when you were married. This will give you time to prepare for the big event. When is it by the way?"

"Ah . . . we haven't decided. Thanks for calling, Linda. Maybe we can get together soon. Bye."

Irritation at Dan for continuing the ruse that they were going to be married edged out Casey's depression.

"When did you decide you wanted to come down to Newport?" Judy pressed her foot to the accelerator and the car picked up speed to pass a long truck hauling logs.

"I don't know. Newport is quaint and lovely. I can afford to spend two or three weeks before I start looking for a job and I thought I'd enjoy the solitude. The tourist season is almost over and I should be able to find a place that's quite reasonable."

Casey felt better now that she was actually on her way. The back seat of the car was loaded with clothes, books, her small TV set, and an assortment of linens she thought she might need if she rented a small housekeeping apartment. The windows of the car were open and Judy's short hair flew in all directions. Casey wore a three-cornered scarf tied tightly at the nape of her neck. It kept her hair pressed to her forehead and covered her ears.

"Look at the size of those cherries," Judy exclaimed. "I want some before I leave, even if they're freighted up from California."

The sign said: "Cherries, Gas, Cottage for rent." Judy turned into the driveway and half an hour later the "for rent" sign was taken down. The gas station and fruit market were run by a retired couple from Salem. Four cabins were set among the trees and Casey rented the one on the end. It was a one-room efficiency and bath, rustic, but comfortable and only a couple of blocks from the beach.

"I wish I was staying a week," Judy said after they unloaded the car. "However, it could be that on the bus ride back to Portland I'll meet a handsome stranger with wide shoulders, a narrow waist, and bulging thighs."

"Don't count on it."

"I won't. He saw you first."

"I told you I don't want to hear one more word about Dan Murdock!"

Judy stayed until Monday morning and they drove into Newport where she took a bus to Corvallis. After shopping at the supermarket, Casey drove back to the cabin and parked the car in the carport. By the time she unloaded her groceries and put them away she was exhausted. She was thankful that she could lie down on the bed and take a nap if she wanted to and there would be no one to bother her.

Tuesday and Wednesday slipped by. Casey lounged in the sun in front of the cabin, went for short walks on the beach, and read three paperback novels. She made occasional trips to the stand for a newspaper or a bag of fruit and carefully avoided going beyond the "Hello, how are you?" stage with the owners and the other occupants of the resort. She had seen the cashier looking at her hands when she paid for her purchases and had almost expected her to murmur, "Oh, you poor thing," or something equally as pitying. She wasn't strong enough to face that yet, so she beat a hasty retreat to her cabin.

Wednesday had been her worst day. Try as she might, she couldn't get the thought out of her mind that this was the day Dan returned from Japan. After he left she had convinced herself his leaving had been a good way for him to break off the visits to the hospital. He had already signed the necessary papers to take care of the doctor and hospital costs. She had to admit it was considerate of him to pay without a hassle between her insurance company and his. He had told her that it was a cut and dried case, and his company would pay.

Sometime during the day, she decided that Dan was a consummate actor, if there ever was one. He had seemed so sincere, so gentle. She could have easily fallen in love with him if she had been exposed to his charm much longer. Ha! She snorted in self-disgust for even thinking about him. He could be another Eddie Farrow, for all she knew, with a wife and six kids waiting at home.

By the end of the week Casey was walking into town and back without exhausting her strength. She found a health food store and bought a mixture of nut meats, raisins, and whole grains to munch on. No one paid much attention to the slim girl in the soft, faded jeans and baggy sweat shirt, with the scarf tied over her hair and a floppy hat tilted over her eyes. The weather was still warm during the day. It was past the first of September and school had started, so the tourists came now only on the weekends.

With calm precision Casey carefully made plans for what she was going to do with her life. In a few weeks she would go to Salem or Corvallis and scan the want ads for work. She didn't particularly care what it was, just something to support her while she waited for the series of operations that would take the scar from her face and replace the missing portion of her ear lobe.

When not working, she decided, she would use

her spare time to sew clothes to sell in a shop she planned to open in one of the small coastal resort towns. Handmade garments sold for premium prices and she was an excellent seamstress. She had made her own clothes, even her jeans with her own label, for years. She liked clothes and knew she had a knack for adding special touches that made them unique. Casey spent hours each day going through fashion magazines, making notes and sketches. Now that she had a goal, the world looked brighter, and she was positive in time she wouldn't even remember dark gray eyes, a square jaw, and a nose that leaned slightly to one side.

The weekend tourists left and the town and beach were quiet once again. Casey was walking several miles a day by the middle of the week. Her self-esteem rose as the exercise and good food strengthened her body. She would survive this traumatic experience just as she and her mother had survived when Eddie left them and as she had survived her mother's death when she was a confused teenager.

On Friday she drove into town to stock up on groceries for the weekend. She bought a new novel by her favorite author and several magazines. As she watched the stores opening for the weekenders she felt increasingly confident that she could make a custom-made clothing shop pay off.

In the evening after showering and preparing for bed, she slid her long slim body between the sheets and opened her new novel.

She was so engrossed in the story that the sound of a sharp rap on the door startled her badly. She sat up in bed as the rap came again.

"Yes. Who is it?" she called and reached for the robe on the end of the bed.

"Phone call." The voice was low and muffled and she wasn't sure she'd heard those words.

Casey belted her robe and glanced in the mirror to pull her bangs down over her forehead and to make sure her ear was covered.

"Did you say phone call?"

"Yes'm."

Something terrible must have happened for Judy to be calling at this time of night, she thought wildly and hurried to unbolt the door. She flung it open and the back of her hand flew to her mouth, her eyes became enormous, and a cold shiver crept down her spine.

Dan stood on widespread legs, those long, muscular legs encased in faded jeans, his hands jammed in the pockets of a worn denim jacket. His dark eyes held hers and from his expression she thought he might grab her and shake her. But when he spoke, his voice was even, almost impersonal.

"I just moved in next door and I'd like to borrow a cup of sugar."

Five

"Dan," Casey whispered, staring wide-eyed up into his face.

"Casey. my darling." There was a curiously sooth-ing quality in his words, as if he were calming her, quieting her the way he had done on the night she woke with her eyes bandaged.

Casey shook her head. "What are you doing here?"

He came into the room, closed the door, and leaned against it. "I've come to get my Guinevere," he said simply.

"You've got to be out of your mind."

"You're repeating yourself, sweetheart. You've told me that before."

"Dan, listen to me," she pleaded, gazing up at him with anxious determination. "I've got enough worries in my life right now, trying to get my strength back, finding a job, starting a new life, without interference from you." She was highly conscious of his physical strength and the patience in his eyes as they swept over her. "I have my life planned, Dan, and you're not part of it."

He pushed himself away from the door. It hardly seemed that he had moved, but there he was looming over her. He appeared to be larger, more rugged, almost primitive.

"What makes you so sure of that?" he asked with a hint of a smile.

"I have my own life to live and it would never in a hundred years be compatible with yours." He laughed and she wanted to hit him. "Stop laughing," she snapped. Her eyes searched his face in puzzlement. "Why? Why are you pursuing this relationship? You hardly know me!"

"Hardly know you?" He looked thoughtful for a moment while his fingers came up and fingered a strand of her hair. "It's true that I haven't known you for a long time. But it's been long enough for me to know that you're intelligent, witty, have a capricious personality, and that I would never be bored with you in a million years." His dark eyes lit up with mischievous delight. "I found myself attuned to you right from the start. Does that sound as if I hardly know you?"

Casey's features took on a look of carved stone, her clear tawny-gold eyes grew cold and unseeing. "If you're looking for a new partner for an interlude of sexual fun and games, forget it. It's not my style."

His long fingers curved around her chin, forcing her to face him. "Believe me, Casey. An 'interlude' with you never crossed my mind." His hands moved lightly over her shoulders. "I don't know where to touch you." He groaned. "And God knows, I want to!" He watched her face closely to see if she winced when his hands moved down her back.

Casey watched his mouth moving toward hers and instinctively splayed her fingers against his chest. Then his mouth deliberately took slow, sensual possession of hers and her lips parted invitingly beneath his, as if she had no control over them. She inhaled the heady fragrance of his aftershave and her tongue tasted the fresh flavor of his mouth. His breathing was ragged and she could feel the pounding of his heart even though he was holding her lightly against him. His hands moved down her back and over her hips, caressing, while his mouth pressed against her with a hungry urgency. Her rapidly disintegrating common sense told her she was treading on dangerous ground and had better act while she could.

"Dan . . . please," she managed thickly. Then as his hand moved from the nape of her neck to push the hair back from her face, she uttered a sharp, "Don't do that!" She jerked herself away from him and turned her back. Nervous hands smoothed the hair around her face.

He was behind her, close, his hands on her upper arms. "Casey," he said in a voice that rasped with emotion. "Surely you know I didn't follow you here for a one night stand." He pressed his cheek against her smooth one. She could hear the scrape of his whiskers on her cheek and the pounding of his heart against her back. His mouth traced a pattern along her jaw line. "I want you to be well and strong when I make love to you. I don't think I'll always be gentle, my Guinevere."

"Please stop calling me that." A distant part of Casey's mind was aware that she was succumbing to an uncontrollable desire to lean back against him, to let his strength support her. "You know there was no Camelot, no Guinevere," she said desperately, striving to put some reality into the situation.

"Who says there wasn't a Camelot? There was a Sir Lancelot and there was a Guinevere, just like there's a Santa Claus and a tooth fairy if we believe it." His hands turned her to face him. "Don't be frightened by this," he murmured. "It's new to me, too. Until a few short weeks ago, I never expected to become involved with anyone, to spend all my waking moments thinking about someone. I had to come here to be with you for awhile and find out what it is about you that fascinates me so. It's as simple as that." His hands slid to either side of her waist. "Does it hurt you when I hold you here?"

"No," Casey whispered. "I only have two really sore spots left."

"Your breast and your ear?" She nodded, her eyes still caught by his. "I'll be careful of them." His voice deepened and his dark eyes never left her gold ones until he lowered his head and his mouth claimed hers with a gentle stamp of ownership. Casey stood quietly with her eyes closed. He traced her upper lip with the tip of his tongue before he raised his head to look at her. He took her hands and brought them up to his neck. "Kiss me once, m'lady," he said huskily, then, "Your hands are cold, get back into bed."

Casey kissed him gently on the lips, then pulled away to look at him. She wanted to say something that made her action sensible. But the truth was she had done it purely in reaction to his request. You're making a mistake, her mind screamed. You're getting in deeper and deeper. Use some common sense and tell him to leave. All you have to do is stay firm, she told herself.

He moved quickly and swung her up in his arms.

"Dan . . .!"

Without a word he carried her to the bed and laid her down. His big hand grasped her bare foot. "Your feet are like ice. Why didn't you say something?" He rubbed first one foot and then the other between his large palms until she could feel the warmth begin to return.

She lay as if in a trance until he reached up to untie the belt of her dressing gown. "No! No . . . don't!" She grabbed at his hands and he straightened and looked down at her.

"I'd never hurt you. You must believe that." There was a world of feeling in the murmured words and against her will she felt them pull at her heart.

"I . . . don't want it off."

"Okay," he said patiently. "But get under the covers." He picked up the novel and placed it on the table, then pulled the covers up over her. Her eyes widened in alarm when he began to remove his jacket. "I'm starving. I hope you've got some food in the refrigerator." He threw his jacket on the end of the bed and went into the kitchenette. His large body seemed to fill it. "I didn't have time to stop if I was going to find this place before dark," he went on with great calm. He brought out the cheese, bread, and some eggs and placed them on the counter. "I'll have a cheese omelet. Want one?" He bent to bring a pan from beneath the counter and didn't see the negative shake of her head. "Just what I need. Nothing cooks an omelet like an iron skillet. What? No toaster? Oh, well, I like my bread buttered and put under the broiler just as well. A little more trouble, though. But remember that."

Casey watched him, smiled a little at the careful way he broke the eggs. Then like a thunderbolt it struck her how relaxed she was and how natural it seemed to have him here. She wondered what it was about this man that made her so leery of him, even though he inspired so much confidence. He was no stranger to the stove. She could tell by the way he poured a small amount of oil in the skillet, grasped the handle with a towel and tilted it so the hot oil could slide over the surface.

Later, whistling under his breath, he turned

the skillet over a plate and dumped a high, fluffy omelet onto it. He grinned proudly.

"Usually when I try to show off my culinary skills everything goes wrong. This must be my lucky day." He cut out a wedge, lifted it to a plate, and then walked over to the bed. "Try this, m'lady," he said with a courtly bow and smiled mischievously. It was impossible for Casey not to respond.

"Aye, m'lord," she said and lowered her lashes demurely. "If only thy skill with the sword equaled thy skill with the skillet." She raised laughing eyes to his.

He placed the plate on the bed beside her. "I am also skilled at slapping bottoms of mouthy maidens, m'lady." He straightened and winked at her. "Should the occasion arise, it would be a most pleasurable task."

Casey's laughter broke free of its own accord. The whole idea of them behaving like this without any of the usual undertones of aggression and conflict struck her as ridiculous. It must be the atmosphere in this place, she mused. She didn't know why, but she felt comfortable and relaxed. In fact she had never felt more safe or more comfortable in her life. It was as if she had been carrying a hollow spot inside of her and suddenly it was filled. She didn't understand it and didn't want to analyze it, just enjoy it. She shoved the thought aside. Like Scarlett, she would think about it tomorrow.

"Want more?" Dan sat on the chair beside the bed holding his plate.

"No. I didn't really want that, but it smelled so good I couldn't resist. I thought you were going to make toast."

"I am when I finish this."

"Why didn't you make it to eat with the omelet?"

"I eat one thing at a time. When I finish this, I'll make the toast. Do you have any honey?"

"No. I don't have much of a sweet tooth."

"I don't for desserts, but honey's different. It's good for you."

"Are you a health food nut?"

"Uh-huh. So are you."

"How do you know?"

"Careful deduction, my dear Watson. I saw the fruit, vegetables, nuts, and natural grain cereal in your fridge."

"Clever."

"I'm no dummy. Give me your plate and I'll make you some toast."

"None for me, thanks, but help yourself."

Later he turned on the small portable TV set, tuned it, and then stretched out on the foot of the bed as if it were his perfect right.

"We'll watch the news and then I'll go so you can get a good night's sleep." He had washed the dishes and tidied up the kitchen. "Tomorrow we'll find a meat market and buy a couple of rib eyes and later you'll dine on a meal fit for a queen."

Casey swallowed hard, and before thinking too much about it, said, "How long are you staying here?"

"Oh, I don't know. Are you tired of me already?"

Quite the reverse, she thought. Aloud, she said, "I haven't thought about it. How did you find me? Judy was the only one who knew where I was and while I didn't exactly tell her I was hiding, she knew I didn't want to see anyone."

"She told me, but don't be mad at her. I camped on her doorstep and threatened to tell someone named Glen that I was her husband." He laughed. "She's a saucy little wench."

"That was unfair," Casey said, but smiled.

"It worked. She told me just how to get here, among other things." He grinned in such a way, she wondered about the other things.

"Has she sublet my apartment?"

"It's taken care of for six months. By that time you'll want to use it again. The way the doctor explained it to me, you'll need a series of operations, but not all of them will require a stay in the hospital."

They were quiet for a long while. Dan watched the news, but Casey was too preoccupied to pay attention to it. The commentator signed off and the weather report came on. Dan laid his head on his arm and looked up the length of her body to her face. His hand searched and found her foot. She could feel the warmth of his hand through the covering and a small shiver of apprehension traveled the length of her spine.

"How was your trip?" The relief was enormous when the words came out evenly.

"It was going along fine until I called and found out you'd checked out of the hospital."

"You called from . . . Japan?" she stammered, shocked and slightly elated that he would go to the expense to call her from so very far away.

"Surely you knew I'd call. I called you before when I was in Mexico." He raised himself up and rested on his bent elbow.

"Mexico?" she echoed.

"The second time I ever called was from Mexico." He paused. "Why didn't you wait until I came back to leave the hospital? The few extra days of care would have been good for you."

She was almost frightened by the quiet strength in his face, but not too frightened to answer back. "I didn't need your permission to check out of the hospital, and I don't need you telling me what is good for me." She braced herself as she saw his face change. It changed, not to anger, but to sheer amusement. Then he burst into hardy laughter. "And that's another thing about you that irritates me," she snapped. "You laugh at the most inappropriate times!"

"I can't wait for my brothers to meet you," he said, still laughing. He inched his way up the bed until he lay beside her, elbow bent, his cheek resting on his palm. She rolled her head on the pillow to look at him. The dark eyes and sensuous mouth were far too close.

"I doubt very much if that will ever happen." She wanted to say "Get off my bed," but that would let him know just how much she was bothered by his closeness.

"We won't go into that now." He brought his face to hers until their noses touched, then drew back to look at her. "I love to look at your eyes. They remind me of the golden eyes I once saw on a kitten, all round and gold-flecked and . . . wary that I was going to hurt it. But I wouldn't have. Not for anything in the world would I have hurt that kitten." His voice lowered in an imitation of a purr.

The touch of his arm against her stomach caused her flesh to tingle and brought a glow to her face. She felt again the warmth and sense of connection that had pulsed so powerfully between them the night in the hospital when he had soothed her with the warm pressure of his hand on her arm. With his eyes still holding hers, his hand moved and lay lightly on her uninjured breast. Oh, God! What was she to do? He was so gentle . . . so sweet. If only she'd met him before and could have cradled his head to her breast and loved him. Loved him? Oh, no! She was in love with him! She'd never dreamed it could hit her like this. She'd never even imagined that love could come with such a force! She wanted to reach out and say, I'm so tired, Dan. Take care of me, love me . . . like I love you. But she didn't. She lay quietly knowing he could feel the thumping of her heart beneath his hand.

"I wish I didn't have to go." His head was on the

pillow beside hers and he whispered the words in her ear. "I could sleep right here," he said as if talking to himself. "But I'm afraid I'd grab you in the night and hurt you," he sighed in her ear. "You are a temptress, m'lady. And if I wasn't the honorable knight that I am, I would ravish you." His tongue swirled in her ear and his lips nibbled at the lobe.

"Ravish!" She almost choked on the giggle that bubbled up inside her. "Aren't you being overly dramatic, m'lord?"

"You seek to cool my ardor with ridicule, m'lady? You tempt me sorely to teach you some respect for your lord and master."

Casey's eyes danced as she turned her ear into the pillow to escape his tongue. "That tickles!" Their faces were inches apart. His eyes played with hers, glowing devilishly, and his arm curled warmly across her.

"Would you believe me if I told you that I've never been happier than I am at this moment?" he asked with such totally unexpected vulnerability that she answered him immediately, honestly, without pausing to think.

"Yes. I believe you."

"And you?"

"I'm not exactly . . . sad," she whispered.

He moved his face closer until their noses lay side by side and their lips barely touched. She could feel the touch of his lashes against her brows before his lips moved, ever so slightly, against hers when he spoke.

"That's a start."

Casey lay quietly, knowing she could turn her face away if she wanted to. Nothing else seemed at all important except the feel of his big, hard body against hers, the regular thump of his heartbeat against her upper arm, and this peaceful, relaxed feeling. She felt his smile against her lips.

"You're like that soft, golden kitten. I can almost hear you purr," he said in a husky whisper.

"I can scratch, too," she murmured drowsily.

His hand searched and found hers, and ever so gently he opened her fingers and pressed her palm against his face. Then he rested his forearm between her breasts while his long fingers caressed her neck and cheek. It was such a sweet, simple gesture. It conveyed a deep longing to touch and to be touched. A wave of tenderness for this rough, sometimes overwhelming man flooded Casey's heart. Her fingers moved in small caresses along his jawline to the dark hair around his ears.

He moved his head a fraction until their noses were tip to tip and looked at her with a gladness in his eyes that made her pulse leap. Then his mouth tenderly and almost reverently planted a kiss on her lips. The kiss was of a totally loving nature, exacting an unreserved response from Casey. Later she was to look back on that kiss and remember it as the moment when the independent, self-sufficient Casey she had always been ceased to exist. She would from then on feel empty unless she was with him.

He continued to press soft, tender kisses on her mouth, but he resisted the demanding pressure of her hand on the back of his head to deepen the kisses.

"This is all we can have for now, sweetheart," he whispered, and raised his head to gaze down on her reddened lips and shining eyes.

For a few magical moments Casey completely forgot her fear of personal involvement with this man. She found the feeling of being loved and pampered by him new and exhilarating beyond her wildest fantasies. Closing her eyes against the momentary giddiness, her next sensation was of him rolling away from her and leaving the bed.

She opened her eyes slowly and saw him looking down at her.

"I'll turn off the TV and the lights and lock the door so you don't have to get up." He held out his hand and she put hers in it. "Night, Guinevere."

"Night, m'lord."

He squeezed her hand gently, then switched off the light.

After he was gone she sighed for his absence, and turned her face into the pillow where his head had lain. The lemony scent of his after-shave still lingered. She was dozing contentedly with the memory of firm, warm lips, laughing dark eyes, and a strong arm holding her, when the sound of a key turning in the lock startled her to full awareness.

The door opened. "Don't be afraid. It's just me," she heard Dan say softly. He closed the door and slid the bolt in place. "I took the key with me when I left," he said, coming toward the bed in the darkness. "The bed isn't made up over there and I've no desire to sleep on a bare mattress." He sat down on the edge of the bed and she heard the thump as his shoes hit the floor.

There was a tightness across her chest, a fullness in her throat, but she couldn't utter a word. She lay there, her hands gripping the edge of the robe she still wore, overwhelmed suddenly by the matter-of-fact way he was getting into her bed.

"Dan . . ." She started to get up, but his hand pushed her down.

"Have you still got on that robe? Take it off, sweetheart, and go to sleep. Oooohhh, I'm tired. I feel like I drove a million miles today." He lifted the covers and slid in beside her. "Kiss me goodnight . . . again," he said, his breath warming her lips. His mouth found hers and lingered to kiss it with proprietary ease. "Won't you be too warm in that robe?"

"No."

"Okay. Give me your hand. I didn't want to leave you anyway. When I saw that bare bed it was a good excuse to come back," he admitted. He stretched out on his back, their clasped hands lying between them. "If King Arthur is looking down on his favorite knight, my Guinevere, I think he would be proud of me—good night."

Six

When Casey awoke, she was lying on her side, her head on the edge of the bed and her arm hanging over the side. The first thing she saw was Dan's denim jacket flung over the back of the chair. She wanted to turn over and look at him while he was sleeping. And she also wanted to remain comfortably content and try to solve this dilemma she found herself in. During the night she had wrestled with the question of her own feelings until exhaustion had given her blessed relief. She was still without answers.

Unfortunately, once awake, she couldn't stay still. Her back and leg muscles were screaming to be stretched. Ever so slowly she folded the robe snuggly across her breast and began to ease her feet to the floor. At her first tentative move, she felt Dan stir.

She turned to find him watching her, the slightest smile on his lips and an odd warmth in his dark eyes.

"I'm sorry. I didn't mean to wake you."

"I've been awake for awhile."

A shiver of pure physical awareness chased down Casey's spine. He had slept in his undershorts. The bedcovers hugged his trim waist. Above was a perfectly beautiful torso—wide shoulders with no coarse knots of muscle, just a huge expanse of rippling flesh with a light dusting of black hair on his tanned arms and across his muscular chest. A charmed grin spread over his face causing an instant tightening around her heart. He was a devastatingly virile and attractive man, both physically and mentally and she was blatantly aware of it. It was the first time in her life she had ever experienced such primitive sexual feelings for a man, and she almost groaned aloud—it was the first time she had ever been in love.

"Are you one of those crazy people who wakes up early and immediately jumps out of bed, Casey?" There was a satisfied expression in his eyes when she jerked hers to meet them.

"Yes, I guess so. I'm one of those disgusting creatures who goes to bed with the sun and gets up with it."

"Good girl!" He lifted his arms over his head and stretched until his joints began to pop. He rested his forearms on the top of his head and gripped his elbows with his hands. He stretched first to one side and then the other while Casey watched fascinated. She had an incredible urge to run her hand freely over his body, to test the firmness of that musculature. A growing tension was building inside her and she pushed herself up into a sitting position and swung her legs off the bed.

"Give me a towel, honey, and I'll shower over at the other cabin," he called just before she closed the bathroom door.

She chose a towel from the shelf and tossed it through the partially closed door, then banged it shut. She heard him chuckle and imagined the boyish smirk on his face. *He knew she was attracted to him.* Casey rolled her eyes at her reflection in the mirror and grimaced. Why wouldn't he accept the fact that they were two people coming from entirely different backgrounds? She had nothing to offer him. She groaned. She wasn't experienced enough to be a good sex partner. He could find plenty of women among the groupies that gathered around a well-known athlete to satisfy him physically. So why her? Damn, damn. She had accepted the loneliness of her life and she wasn't going to be so foolish as to accept a casual affair with him now.

She stripped and looked at herself in the full-length mirror on the bathroom door. She may have been scarred from her knees to her shoulders, but she was strong, resilient, and proud. She'd deal with the consequences of this relationship on a day-to-day basis, she told herself firmly as she stepped into the shower and turned the water on full blast.

When she emerged from the bathroom, Dan was coming in the door. He paused and grinned at her, then unfastened his belt and stuffed his knit shirt neatly into the waistband of his Levi's. His torso showed to advantage in the blue knit pullover with the alligator on the pocket. His head was wet and his cheeks smooth. He was a fast dresser for he had accomplished all of this during the time it had taken her to shower, dress, apply makeup, and stare at her reflection in the bathroom mirror.

Casey was totally unaware of the arresting picture she made. Her jeans hugged her tall, curving figure and the green plaid shirt was perfect with her gold hair and eyes. Dan appraised her admiringly, making her aware of her unrestrained breasts beneath the soft cotton shirt. Her fingers went to the top buttons to reassure herself they were closed. She hadn't worn a bra since the accident.

"Are you a dieting woman who merely sips a little coffee for breakfast?" His eyes teased her.

"Sorry to disappoint you. I favor a hardy breakfast."

"Good girl," he said for the second time that morning. "C'mon. I know a place that serves a fantastic breakfast—ham, baking powder biscuits, and gravy."

"Gravy? For breakfast?"

"C'mon. You'll like it."

"What's the weather like?"

"Better take a jacket or a sweater. There's a stiff breeze blowing this morning."

Casey paused to tie the scarf around her head and grab a wrap.

Dan took the keys and they left the cabin. The car he led her to was, after she had time to think about it, ideally suited to him. It was a big car for a big man. Somehow she couldn't picture him crawling into a sports car just inches off the ground and folding himself into a bucket seat. The seats in the car were wide and covered with soft cream leather. It was definitely more luxurious than flamboyant.

"You've been here before?" Casey asked when he turned the car out onto the highway and headed south.

"Many times. I used to dive for abalone around here. My brothers and I would come here several times a year during the season. Ever done any scuba diving?"

"No. But I always thought I'd like to." She wanted to ask him more about his brothers, but before she could think of a way to phrase the question, he told her.

"My brothers have been like two fathers to me since my dad died when I was fourteen. One of them is twelve years older and the other fourteen years older than me. I think I was a happening that my parents didn't expect." He turned and grinned at her. "I was spoiled to a certain extent, but they worked the hell out of me, too. The three of us operate the business, but as I'm the only single one I usually have to do the away from home stuff. I've a feeling that's going to come to a screeching halt."

Casey quickly passed over the meaning of his words and asked a question to cover her distraction.

"Do they have children?"

"Do they have children? I figure Hank's wife has been pregnant more than five years of the sixteen they've been married. They have seven. Fred has only five."

"You don't like kids?" Casey asked with an odd inflection in her voice.

"Sure. What ever gave you that idea? I want a whole parcel. I've already got the house, the dog, and the station wagon." He shot her a wicked sidelong glance that intimated he expected a response.

"Well . . . you didn't sound as if you approved of your brothers' large families," she said lamely.

"I had to grow up by myself. I'd never wish that on another kid." He wheeled the car into the parking lot of a long low building, shut the motor off, and turned to look at her. "You were an only child. Wouldn't you rather have had brothers and sisters?"

"Yes," she said quietly. "An only child has to bear all the responsibility for a sick mother or an errant father. I would have loved to have had a brother or a sister to share that responsibility."

He reached for the hand she had wrapped in the sweater she held in her lap. "I don't think you'll need this yet." He laid the wrap on the back of the seat. "You make me ashamed for complaining about my younger years. At least I had my brothers and then their wives and kids."

Casey pulled her hand away and turned to look out the car window. His sympathy made her feel weak and teary.

"Are we going to eat or not?" She licked her dry lips, regretting she had revealed so much about herself. With nervous fingers she smoothed the hair down over her forehead and lightly touched the scarf to make sure it was over her ears.

After breakfast they drove into Newport, parked the car, and walked the length of the business district, peering into shop windows and looking over the assortment of souvenirs. Casey stopped to peer through the door of a small empty shop. She took her hand from Dan's to cup it around her eyes so she could see inside the empty room. It was paneled with rough wood and the floor was made from wide planks, varnished and waxed. She could easily visualize her shop in such a room as this. Then she looked at the "for sale" sign in the window and knew this place would be out of the question for her.

"Are you planning on opening a fish and bait shop?" Dan teased.

"Fish and bait? Ugh!" He had taken her hand again, and she laughed up at him and suddenly decided that, whatever came later for her, she was going to enjoy this day. She felt unable to deny herself the excitement of being with him in this little rustic resort town. The future would have to take care of itself. "I want to open a shop and sell handmade garments." As they walked slowly down the sidewalk she found herself telling him her ideas for making the clothes during the winter months so she would have an inventory ready for spring. He listened intently.

"You sew that well? Do you make men's shirts?"

"I never have, but I could. I make all my knit pullovers."

"I can't get a shirt that's wide enough in the shoulders that doesn't swallow me around the waist, and usually they aren't long enough to tuck into low-slung jeans."

"That wouldn't be a problem. Take away a little here, add a little there. I'll use you as a model. Better yet, a walking billboard. I'll make a shirt and put a sign on the back and you can stand out in front of the shop."

He chuckled and she caught the devilish glint in the depths of his eyes. "Like a wooden Indian, huh?"

"Something like that."

"Did you make that shirt?"

"Uh-huh. The jeans, too."

He stopped and turned her around. "You're kidding!" He ran his hand down over her hips, then tucked his fingers into the hip pocket. "You've even got a label. CASEY. I've picked myself *some* woman!" Then, as if talking to himself, he added, "She's not only beautiful, but independent, witty, talented, and ambitious."

Casey's face froze and the smile left her eyes. Dan sensed immediately he had said something wrong. "What is it? What did I say to take that happy look off your face?"

"Nothing. Forget it." She started to walk down the street, her hands deep in the side pockets of her jeans, more conscious of the scar on her face than she had been all morning. At the car she waited for him to unlock the door.

Without saying a word he started the motor, turned the car into the stream of traffic, and headed up the coast. They had driven only a short way when he turned down a sandy road toward the beach and pulled to a stop. The Pacific Ocean spread out before them.

"I want to know what turned you off." His hands gripped the wheel and his domineering eyes gleamed through narrowed lids.

"I despise insincere flattery," she said icily.

"Insincere? I meant every word I said," he gritted in an equally intense tone.

"Liar!" she spat. "I've heard my father spout similar lines!"

"Don't ever compare me to Edward Farrow! Or to any other man." Casey could see that he was furious and found herself unable to move as his hands shot out and gripped her shoulders. "I think I know what's in that head of yours." His smoldering look was pinning her to the seat. Her hands clenched together tightly in her lap.

"Stop trying to run my life for me. You have no right—"

"I have a right and you know it whether you admit it to yourself or not. The trouble with you is you're *too* damned proud. I wouldn't go so far as to call you vain, but close to it, Casey. Close."

"I'm not!" she spat. "Stop analyzing me."

"You're afraid for me to see what's under that beautiful veneer," he snapped. "You've been brainwashed by all that feminist propaganda that says it's wrong for a woman to want to merge *her* life with that of a man, share *his* dreams, *his* ambitions, marry and have children. In fact it's the most natural and right thing for a woman to do— along with a lot of other things." He paused and she heard his breath hiss between his teeth. "You're ashamed to admit that it was a comfort to know I was taking care of you in the hospital. You think it's a weakness to depend on me. You've been on your own for so long you're afraid of commitment, especially now that you think your appearance isn't what it was before the accident."

"I know it isn't, and I can live with it. What I don't have to live with is someone saying stupid—"

Dan's mouth, hard and commanding, fastened on her mobile lips, stealing her breath away and swallowing her words. There was nothing gentle about his kiss. He was using his mouth as a means of shutting hers. Casey twisted her head from side to side, but she didn't push against him to free herself. She let his warmth seep into her; she luxuriated in his strength, finding all the comfort and support she could ever want.

The pounding of her heart made her realize that his lips had softened, and that she was cradled in his arms. With a drowning feeling she attempted to push him away. He seemed to be totally unaware of her efforts and merely pulled her closer. Her lips were irresistibly forced apart until the warmth of his mouth made her give up the struggle and her arms slipped up about his neck.

Her surrender seemed to trigger a deeper need in him and the quality of his kiss exploded into a persuasive, sensuous, passionate demand that caused something warm and powerful to throb in the area below her stomach. Fear that she was losing control brought her back to reality.

"Dan, please don't!" she begged when his lips freed her mouth to rest on her cheek.

"Don't say those things to me ever again, Casey." His voice was a deep rumble. He moved his face so that he could look at her. Her eyes were damp and wide and her mouth puffy and trembling. "There's more to you than a pretty face. It's an old cliché, but true when applied to you." His mouth was still set stubbornly and Casey's eyes riveted on it. "I like the way you hold your head, your slender neck. I like your wiry, tight body, your height, the way your hair shines. Most of all I like your eyes that reflect all your emotions. And your mouth. I have never kissed a sweeter mouth." His lips sipped at a tear that rolled down her cheek. "What I don't like is surliness and dishonesty," he said firmly and softened his words with a gentle kiss.

"I don't understand you," she whispered. "I don't understand you at all."

"I don't understand me either. I just know I'm miserable when I'm away from you. I worry that you'll need me and I won't be there. I'm happiest when I'm with you. I knew that the first night in the hospital," he said with great certainty. "I've been honest with you about that."

"You couldn't have made up your mind that fast."

"I did," he said, smiling at her. "Can't we just leave it at that and see what happens?"

She nodded. His words had brought her a delicious breathlessness. This can't last, she told herself sternly. Her mind clicked into gear while she searched his dark eyes, now tender and teasing. As long as she recognized the danger of being terribly hurt at some later date, she might as well give herself up to this reckless, dreamlike interlude.

"Okay," she whispered. "I'm sorry I called you a liar."

"Are you sure?" he asked lightly as he wrapped her in his arms. She cuddled willingly and raised her lips. He kissed her long and tenderly. "C'mon, let's walk on the beach."

They walked for hours along the stony beach, picking up and discarding shells and other treasures the waves had cast up during the night. Sometimes they talked, sometimes they merely shared companionable silence, the sun falling warm and golden on their skin. When Dan thought she was tiring he found a spot protected from the northwest wind by a giant boulder. For a long while they lay on the fine sand sharing confidences, opinions, experiences.

I'm a Democrat. Are you? I don't care much for Country Western music, but I do like Kenny Rogers. I don't like the food in Mexico, but I like it Texas style. I've seen Swan Lake. Me, too. Did you get the drift of the story? Sure. I guess I was too busy watching to see if someone fell off their toes. Oh, you . . .

Sometimes there were short periods of silence, and always some part of Dan was touching her— his hand, his shoulder, his thigh. It was almost as if he couldn't bear not touching her.

Only one thing happened to mar the tranquillity of the day. Casey lay dozing. Dan, leaning on one elbow, explored her throat with his mouth. His fingers found the nipple on her breast and teased it to hardness through the thin cotton of her shirt.

"No bra," he whispered into her ear. "Hummmm . . . I like that." His mouth moved down and his lips replaced fingers that began working on the buttons of her shirt.

The alarm in her brain overcame the delicious feeling of his mouth tugging at the erect bud. She panicked and her hand grabbed his.

"No, Dan! Don't!"

His fingers stopped immediately and he rolled over on his back, away from her. A rush of misery, an overwhelming sense of loss, welled up inside her. She inhaled deeply, knowing she had denied herself the tactile pleasure of being caressed by his strong, male hands. She wanted to take the sharp words back and replace them with

Please, I can't stand for you to see my ugly body.
She didn't know what to do, so she just lay there,
doing nothing. The sun went behind a cloud and
stayed there. Casey shivered, suddenly cold. Her
groping fingers reached for his hand, wanting his
body warmth. He didn't push her away and when
he opened his arms she rolled into them, her
mouth open against his neck.

"It's all right," he whispered, his voice husky,
and she wanted to cry.

Because they had skipped lunch, they decided
to have an early dinner. On the way back to the
cabin they stopped at the supermarket. While Casey
pushed the cart, Dan selected the groceries.

"Don't get so much, unless you plan on stick-
ing around here." She laughed. "I'm leaving on
Monday."

"This food will be long gone by then. I have a
huge appetite."

Back at the cabin, Dan carried the two bags of
groceries into the kitchen.

"What can I do to help?" Casey asked, a little
intimidated by his expertise in selecting the steaks
and the vegetables. What other surprises did he
have in store for her?

"Nothing. This is my production. I don't need
an amateur cook in my way." He grinned at her
and punched her nose with a gentle finger.

Casey smiled up at him, pleased by their ease
with one another. Ease? She was always conscious
of the lean tautness of his body, of the whipcord
strength of his arms, and the pulse throbbing in
his brown throat just below the level of her eyes.

"I'm no dummy," she said saucily. "I can take a
hint."

"Take a shower instead and put on something
soft," he commanded, but with a tenderness in
his eyes that forced her into the humiliating ne-
cessity of having to control her quickening breath.

"M'lady's dinner will be served in about . . ." he consulted the gold watch strapped to his wrist, "one hour."

"What about you?"

"That includes my shower, too. I'll run over and get some clean clothes. I don't want to drop sand in my salad." He smiled into her eyes, the upturning of his lips engagingly boyish.

Under the shower, Casey told herself she wasn't a starry-eyed teenager with unrealistic ideas about romance. Although there was absolutely no doubt that Dan was the only man she had ever met who set her pulse throbbing, it was something else that made her fall in love with him. Although he was a big man, there was something vulnerable about him, something that made her want to gather him in her arms and hold him as if he were a child. Oh, hell! she groaned. Did she dare go to bed with him? Dare to reach for the chance to share that most intimate experience with the man she loved? What if she got pregnant? Was Dan one of those men who was always prepared with birth control devices in the glove compartment of his car? She shuddered, then wrenched off the shower. This was really crazy, she thought.

The closet was a curtained off end of the bathroom. Casey went through the clothes and rejected everything until she came to a blue and green Indian-print caftan with a high banded neck and loose three-quarter-length sleeves. She had made the garment several years before and had worn it many times. It was one of her favorites. She dried her hair and brushed it until it crackled, then arranged it around her face to cover her scar. She skillfully applied a light makeup, added a touch of pink gloss to her lips, and slipped into the caftan. She wouldn't admit even to herself why her hands trembled as she fastened the small covered buttons up to the band at the neck.

Feeling an uncharacteristic shyness, she opened the door and stepped out into the main room. Dan's whistle of appreciation confirmed what her mirror had already told her. He was busy chopping vegetables but laid the knife down and came to her.

"Oh, gorgeous lady, I must have a quick kiss to speed me on my way to the shower." He kissed her lightly on the nose. "You smell good. Better than onions and garlic." He sniffed her neck, inhaling deeply.

"I should hope so!" She laughed. "This is my fifteen-dollar stuff." She hoped he didn't realize her stomach was doing a slow hula dance.

He drew back and they exchanged grins. "You're trying to seduce me!" he said with mock alarm. "Do you plan to dance for your supper?"

"Better that than washing the dishes," she quipped.

"Then don't do a thing until I get back. Sit right here." He eased her down on a stool beside the counter, brought an iced drink from the refrigerator, and placed it in front of her. He picked up a stack of clean clothes, the towel she had given him the night before folded neatly on top, and disappeared into the bathroom.

How strange that the two of them, so opposite in backgrounds and life-styles, could be together like this. Casey was thoughtful as she sipped the iced lime drink. It was almost as if they were married. But if that were the case, they would have showered together. No! Oh, God! She couldn't bear the thought of standing naked beside his beautiful body and have him look at hers, so scarred and ugly.

"Get a grip on yourself, Casey," she whispered out loud. In order to do so, she quickly turned her attention to Dan's meal preparations.

Chopped tomatoes, spinach, and fresh cauliflower sat on the counter. Two thick rib-eye steaks waited to go under the broiler, while a pot on the range exuded a delicate odor she couldn't identify.

Casey pulled the table from the wall and set two places. Dan stood in the bathroom doorway and rubbed his damp hair briskly with a towel. He had a quiet, questing look on his face.

"I can't get over the feeling that you and I have been in a situation like this before. I almost feel as if I should look out the window and see if the Indians are coming."

Casey was startled at the serious note in his voice. "You're not kidding."

"No, sweetheart." He disappeared into the bathroom and came out seconds later with his damp hair brushed smoothly in place. "I feel like I've known you forever."

"Well, I could have been Lucrezia Borgia and you could have been one of my . . . ah . . . victims," she said lightly in an attempt to tease him out of his serious mood. It worked. He smiled and his dark eyes roamed over her.

"What a way to go." He leered.

Dan insisted she sit on the stool and relax while he prepared dinner. He slid the steaks under the broiler. While they sizzled, he tossed the salad and sliced a fat loaf of sourdough bread. He spread the slices with garlic butter and arranged them on a cookie sheet to place under the broiler when the steaks were done.

"Where did you learn to cook like this?" Casey asked curiously.

"In a logging camp when I was about sixteen." He paused to lift the lid and stir the contents of the pot. "You'll love my seasoned rice," he said so smugly that she laughed. "I told you, my brothers worked the hell out of me. They turned me over to the camp cook, an old lumberjack named Joe Keenan. He was the best cook in ten counties and an even better diver for abalone. He taught me how to cook *and* how to dive."

During the meal Dan told her about his younger years. How his brothers would bargain with him—work hard and keep your grades up and you can have a trip, a horse, a car. He was never *given* anything. He worked for wages like the rest of the crew.

"What I learned in the logging camps was—never make excuses, shoulder your load, and don't back down from a bully." They exchanged smiles across the table. "I got my nose broken more than once."

"Oh, so that's what moved it slightly off center. I thought it was from playing rugby." Casey felt deliciously wicked. Her tawny-gold eyes danced and her delicate mouth smiled mischievously.

Dan touched his nose with his thumb and forefinger. "Don't you like my nose?" He raised his brows haughtily.

"I like it. But . . . it could be more . . . ah . . . this way." She held her hand close to his face and made like jerky movements to the side.

His hand snaked out and grasped hers. "Woman! You're cruisin' for a bruisin'!" He flashed her a wide, happy smile.

They did the clean-up together. Casey was surprised at how neat he was. All the utensils he used were washed and dried and put back in exactly the places he had found them. The towels were left spread on the edge of the counter to dry.

"What shall we do now, m'lady?" he said lightly and studied her face in the overhead light. Suddenly he reached up and switched it off, but he continued to look searchingly at her in the romantic glow from the table lamp.

"What do you suggest?" She suddenly felt dwarfed by his aggressive maleness hovering over her. She stared up at him with wide eyes.

"Right now I'd just like to kiss you," he said huskily and drew her to him.

Seven

Dan leaned against the counter, his long legs spread wide. He drew her between them and pressed her against him intimately. His lips sipped at her neck, even now being careful of her ear. They moved around to kiss the scar on her cheek.

"Dan! No!" She gasped, her hands going to his chest to push him away.

"You say that word an awful lot." He was kissing her throat just behind her ear, and refusing to allow her to move away from him. "Mmmm, your hair is as feathery and soft as the wing of a wood duck," he murmured, nuzzling it again. "Smells good, too."

"Dan . . . please . . ."

"I want to make love to you." His lips moved to her face, his hands to her hips. "I want to love you here in this cabin, as I feel I've loved you before, with the wolves howling at the door and the Indians just over the next ridge." Their breaths mingled as his lips hovered over hers.

Under his stroking hands, Casey's body went slack with sensuousness, pressing softly against him. Her arms went up around his neck, her fingers twisting in the rough black hair at the nape. His lips rubbed seductively against hers and desire flooded her mind, obliterating all reason. She was ready for him and wondered wildly how she could so easily shake off her qualms about making love without commitment. Hungrily, blindly, she sought his mouth, and her kiss conveyed the deep heat in her body which was about to flare out of control. Whatever the future held, she thought, tonight belonged to her and Dan. One night out of a lifetime wasn't asking too much. Whatever the consequences, she'd meet them later. She wasn't going to deny herself the ecstatic pleasure of being caressed by this big, gentle man. His mere touch stirred wanton lusts she hadn't dreamed she was capable of experiencing.

"Sweetheart?" He lifted his head. His eyes were filled with an intense expression. She saw hunger, lust, possession, and something more, much more . . . loving concern for her. It stopped her breath. "Oh, sweetheart . . ."

His arms, like rigid bands, closed about her and she could feel the evidence of his want, firm and hard, against her. She throbbed with responsive want, with the urgent need to be filled. Their mouths met with equal fervor—hot, searching, insistent. She clutched him to her, desperate in her desire to possess and be possessed.

"Darling . . .!" Her mouth moved a fraction and the word came from the center of her being.

"Am I, sweetheart? Am I your darling?" his voice was hoarse. His eyes were very close and flared with warmth. Little flecks of green seemed to float in the dark gray, like atoms around the black nucleus of his pupil. Her own amber eyes were caught by his and a half smile hovered at his mouth.

Casey's mind suddenly snapped alive. Had she really uttered that word? With a deep breath, she hid her face against his neck. "Yes, you are my darling," she whispered. "Please turn off the lamp."

"Mmmm . . . you taste like fresh peach ice cream." His lips made small nibbles along the side of her neck.

Casey turned in his arms and would have moved away, but he held her back pressed to his chest. "Turn off the lamp," she said desperately.

His large hands covered her stomach, which drew in at the touch of his fingers. He made circling movements. The caftan slid smoothly over her skin.

"Is it so important?" he whispered in her ear. His fingers moved lower and pressed against the cushioned bone between her thighs . . . pressed firmly, thrillingly until her buttocks were tight against the zipper of his jeans.

"Yes. Don't make me beg . . ." she said with a muffled groan.

He released her instantly and she turned and leaned on the counter so she didn't see him cross the room to the lamp on the table beside the bed. She closed her eyes and when she opened them the room was dark and the soft rustle told her Dan was undressing. Her hands went to the buttons on the caftan, but she was trembling so much it was difficult to undo them. Then he was turning her and she leaned against warm skin and silky chest hair. Casey felt an odd glow, a small swelling sensation, somewhere between the legs that parted to welcome the intrusion of a muscular thigh.

"It's been so . . . long . . ." she whispered into the curve of his neck.

"Thank God," he murmured against her dewy

skin. His mouth found hers and he kissed her long and deep while a thumb feathered her cheek. His hand smoothed over the fabric that covered her. "How do I get you out of this?" he asked anxiously.

Casey moved back from his arms and pulled the garment over her head and let it fall to the floor. Instantly his hands were on her waist pulling her back to him, her softness against his hardness. The thick, crinkly brush on his chest tickled her breast before cushioning it. His hands roamed her back and slid into the thin panties that covered her hips.

"Ahhh!" He eased away the only barrier between them. "You feel so . . . wonderful. It's like I've waited all my life for this." The panties fell to the floor; she stepped out of them and her high heeled slings.

There were a hundred reasons why she shouldn't be doing this, but she was in such a passionate frenzy that nothing mattered except Dan. No man had kissed her and caressed her like this. No man had ever awakened the sleeping passion that Dan had awakened. None of this should have happened, but now that it had, she was fiercely happy. In the safety of the darkness she slid her arms about his neck and pressed herself to him. Her face was raised to his, and he took her mouth, teased it with his tongue, parted her lips, and let his tongue mingle with hers. He moaned into her open mouth, one large hand on her back, the other on her hips pressing her flat stomach to his, the evidence of his passion hot and hard between them.

"Will I hurt you, darling, if I pick you up?" he whispered, his mouth so close to hers that she could feel the warmth of his breath on her wet lips. She thought crazily that he tasted of sweet mint tea.

"No," she said softly. "No one has picked me up, but you, since I was a little girl."

Dan bent slightly and his arm came beneath her knees. Both her arms were about his neck and he lifted her high against his chest. He stood holding her and her hands moved over the smooth muscles of his shoulders and down his back. It was one of the most wonderously exciting moments of her life. He was holding her tenderly, cradled in his arms as if she were a small child, but the kisses he placed on her shoulders and neck were the kisses of a man desperate to make love. He moved across the room and sat down on the edge of the bed, then turned and lay down with her still in his arms. Her head was in the crook of his arm and she couldn't have moved even if she had wanted to.

"I want our first time to be long and sweet until you ache for me." His voice was deep, soft.

He began to stroke her, his hands moving from shoulder to hip; he whispered love words, their meaning lost to her as he kissed her soft breast, her shoulders and neck, burying his face in the curve. The powerful tug of her own desire set her ablaze with a hunger equal to his. There was no haste in his lovemaking. Sensuous, languid, he took his time quite deliberately, and every move he made was to increase her sexual excitement. He was invading every inch of her now, exploring her body boldly, making her give herself up to him. His breathing suddenly became harsh and she could feel him tremble against her, and felt a shock of eager excitement to know that he was aroused to the point of no return.

"Darling . . . sweetheart . . ." His breath was ragged in her ear. "Are you ready for me? I . . . can't wait much longer!"

"You don't have to wait, darling." Her hand

moved down the smooth skin of his side and across the flat stomach muscles and grasped him.

His response was so convulsive that Casey was almost frightened. He writhed against her and trembled violently, his mouth everywhere on her face, his hands searching for her moist depth. He growled deeply in his throat when she twined her leg over his catching him between her thighs.

"I don't want to be rough . . . I don't want to hurt you," he breathed desperately. "But . . ."

The next minute she was on her back. He leaned over her, sought entrance, and filled her completely. The pain-pleasure was so intense that she cried out his name. Now she was only female body responding to powerful male body. He probed urgently, turning this way and that, while she arched to impale herself more completely on his throbbing warmth.

"Oh, darling! Oh, my God! We fit so perfectly. Oh, love . . ." He moaned with pleasure while resting on his elbows, and Casey locked her arms about him and pressed her lips to his mouth. "Sweetheart . . ."

A heavenly feeling began to build as Dan's motions grew more and more frantic. She wanted what they were reaching for desperately, dreaded missing it, and quivered with expectation beneath the pressure of his body. She clung to him, heedless of sore spots now, aware only of that thrusting, pulsing rhythm increasing unbearably to a tempo that brought her higher . . . higher. She felt deep, thrilling spasms, exquisite pleasure. From somewhere in the blaze, she heard a soft triumphant, "Oh, God!"

Casey came languidly back to reality and found her hands clasping Dan's tight buttocks, his hair on her cheek as he rested face down. He was still huge and deep inside her, but the waves of frenzied pleasure that had ripped through her were subsiding. In their place swelled a burning desire to comfort and pleasure him. She moved her hands over his back and turned her lips to his cheek. His heart was still thundering against hers when he wrapped his legs around her and turned on his side, taking her with him.

They lay face to face, her soft belly tight against his hard one. His hand moved along the length of her from her thigh up over her hip past her waist and beyond to her injured breast. He had just barely touched it and her hand grasped his wrist and moved it away. He was still for a long moment, then rolled her over him and they lay on their other sides. His hand moved to her breast and she brought her hand up and pressed it there. She began to tremble and her lips moved over his chin to his mouth.

They kissed for a long time, as if it were the first time they had kissed, as if there couldn't be anything beyond a kiss, a kiss that had to be all they could have. His tongue was inside her mouth and moving softly and slowly while his fingers teased the nipple on her breast. Then his fingers drifted lightly down to her belly, and fluttered their way between their flesh to where soft curls nestled among his own crisp hair.

"Is it blond?" he asked against her mouth.

"Yes," she whispered and his hand went to her buttocks to press her more tightly to him before moving back to her breast, lifting and holding it until his mouth could reach her nipple. He tugged on it with his lips, gently at first, then almost roughly. The varieties of pressure thrilled her in different ways and in her belly and deep, deep inside of her. The feeling was so acutely pleasurable that she sighed and tightened her arms about him, and he laughed deep in his throat. He lifted his head and pressed her wet nipple to his and moved it gently, teasing it against the rough hair on his chest.

His lips moved from her mouth to her eyes. "Are your eyes open, my love? I wish I could see them. You're so incredibly sweet! I want you to feel everything!"

"If I felt any more . . . I'd explode," she murmured, and he chuckled.

His hand lifted her breast again. "You tie me in knots, woman." He lowered his head to take her breast into his mouth and worry the taut nipple with his tongue.

"Mmmmmmmmmmm." She arched against him and he began to move gently. "Dan . . ."

"Talk to me, darling." His hands were everywhere, his lips nibbling at hers. "Tell me how you feel, what you want, although I'm sure we've done this a million times before."

Her hands moved over his firm, muscled body. "Ahhhh . . ." The sound came from deep in his throat when her fingers found a bud on his chest and massaged it. "There's nothing more wonderful than the feel of you surrounding me. Oh! Lie still, darling!" he breathed in gasps when she began to move. "Forgive me," he whispered, and with a long breath he thrust at her full force and incredibly her body responded to him and they merged into a long, long, unbelievably beautiful release to the accompaniment of their moans of pleasure. Then they lay shuddering in each other's arms.

Casey's arms curved about him tenderly. She had an odd sense of power. This big, self-assured man had quivered in her arms as she had in his.

Slowly his breathing steadied, and he turned on his back to lie beside her, his arm pulling her to him, his hand bringing her thigh up to rest on his. They were quiet for a long while and his fingers moved back and forth over her thigh.

"Do you think the Indians will attack tonight?" Casey whispered and suppressed a giggle. She felt the silent chuckle resound in his chest.

"They could have stormed the cabin, sweetheart, and I'd have been helpless as a babe." His lips found her forehead. "I think you were a witch in your other life."

"Then I shall get on my broomstick and fly away."

"Never!" he said firmly and moved her up in the bed so he could cover them with the sheet. "Go to sleep, love. I've got to plow the south forty tomorrow."

"And I've got to spin some wool to make you a shirt," she quipped.

Tucking the covers around them he cuddled her warm body against his and almost instantly he was asleep.

Feeling wonderfully loved and happily relaxed, Casey closed her eyes thinking she would wait until he was sleeping soundly before she got up to put on her gown and robe.

Then she, too, was asleep.

Coming out of a deep sleep, Casey was aware of teasing fingers between her thighs and lips fastened softly to her breast. She came half awake and realized she was lying on her back and Dan's head lay on her breast. Her arm tightened about him, and swiftly and silently he pulled her legs about him and embedded himself in her moistness. Involuntarily she constricted about him, and with a muffled cry he stiffened and thrust deeply. In minutes they were panting in each others' arms. Casey had never felt so completely a woman. He pressed his head into the hollow of her shoulder.

"Casey, darling, I love you," he whispered.

She held him until the deepness of his breathing told her he was sleeping soundly, then she eased him out of her arms and got slowly out of bed. In the darkness she felt her way to the bathroom door, went inside and closed it before she turned on the light. She stood with her back to the door and allowed her eyes to become used to the harsh brightness. She turned and looked at herself in the mirror. She almost cringed away from the image she saw there. Her disheveled hair was pulled back. The scar and the ear with part of the lobe missing seemed to be all she could see in the face that stared back at her. Deliberately she forced her eyes lower to the skin of her stomach and thighs and to her injured breast. Tears sprang to her eyes.

She turned from the mirror and quickly washed herself and slipped into a high-necked cotton gown with three-quarter sleeves. Judy had bought it for her to wear in the hospital. She felt *safe* behind the gown. She looked at her image once more and picked up the hairbrush and arranged her hair around her face. Now, she thought, most of the ugliness was hidden.

Casey turned out the light in the bathroom and stood for a moment before she quietly turned the knob and opened the door. The light from the lamp beside the bed illuminated the room and she stood hesitantly in the doorway until Dan's eyes swung toward her and then she moved toward the bed.

He lay on his back with his hands clasped behind his head. The covers that had been tucked so neatly beneath the mattress at the foot of the bed were pulled out and his feet hung over the edge. His large frame took up more than half the bed and she wondered almost idly if she had really lain in the small space that was left. A corner of the cover was thrown carelessly across his hips barely covering the thick mat of hair below his flat belly.

Casey was suddenly very nervous, oddly tense. She walked on stiff legs to the bed and stood looking down at him. Her eyes drank in everything about him—the beard that was beginning to show on his cheeks, the lock of hair on his forehead, the incredible strength of his arms and shoulders, his wide mouth and the quietness of the gray-black eyes that looked up at her. Her nose quivered with the scent of male body, with overtones of antiperspirant and after-shave, and the enticing sensual smell of their lovemaking.

"I thought you were asleep."

"I woke the second you left my arms."

"Oh." She was suddenly conscious that her breast ached and smarted and that she was sore between her thighs, but more than that she was conscious of the fact she wanted to be back in his arms. He grinned up at her, his eyes warm, and so loving that she felt her body inclining eagerly toward him. He reached up and gathered her gently, not passionately, to him.

"Why did you leave me to put this on?" His big hand plucked at the sleeve of the nightgown. "Are you shy, my Guinevere?"

"I thought we were living our frontier life and I was your Clementine?" She curled against him like a contented kitten.

He chuckled. "This gown looks like one my Clementine would own. If you insist on wearing one, I'll have to buy you a twentieth-century gown. But I like it much better if there's nothing between us." His hand passed over her breast and she flinched at the soreness. "Sweetheart . . . this isn't your injured one." He paused, frowning. "Did I rough you up too much? I'm sorry. You're a powerful temptation. You're so desirable you bring out the beast in me." He touched the tip of her nose with his lips. "Has it been a *very* long time, darling?" he whispered with a slight catch in his voice.

She decided to be honest. "I had an affair when I was eighteen, but I broke it off when I saw I was heading down the same primrose path my mother had taken. Five years ago I had a one-night experience and decided I'd rather remain celibate than go through that again."

There was a long silence while she wondered if she had revealed too much. His hand moved up under the wide sleeve of her gown and he stroked her shoulder and back. It was as if the two of them were alone in the world. Finally, as if compelled, Dan put his fingers beneath her chin and raised her face so he could look down into her eyes.

"Did what happened tonight put you off again?"

Casey felt her breath catch in her throat, felt her insides warm with pleasure as she looked into the quiet face and dark eyes now anxiously waiting her answer. Love and tenderness welled within her. She lifted her hand and held it to his cheek. He had been more open, more honest with her than any person she had ever met. No games, no pretense. He had said he wanted to get to know her. But how was he to know that she would fall so desperately in love with him? If only she had met him before the accident. Now she couldn't bear to see the revulsion in his eyes if he looked at her naked body. He might think he loved her now, but later . . .

"Dan." She told herself she mustn't cry. "Darling, it was the most wonderful experience of my life." Her warm, moist lips traced the line of his brow and delicately closed his eyelids, then worked their way downward, touching his cheek and the tip of his nose; they settled very gently on his mouth where they moved with sweet provocation. Such a lovely feeling unfolded in her midsection and traveled slowly throughout her body that she wanted it to go on and on. It was strange to her, this feeling of wanting to give and give and give to him, wanting to comfort and cherish him. She had never known this melting, letting-go sensation that now invaded her innermost being. Never before had anyone penetrated the personal barrier she had built to protect herself from emotional pain.

Dan lay quietly in her arms. He seemed to be clinging to *her*, needing assurance from *her*. A fierce feeling of protectiveness came over her and she hugged his head to her breast and smoothed the hair back from his eyes. She would have been content to lie there forever. They didn't talk. And caressing him no longer made her feel shy; it seemed to be the natural thing to do.

"Darling . . . we didn't use a contraceptive. . . ." His voice came from beneath her chin. The covers had slipped down around their knees and he lay in her arms like a naked babe. "I could have. I have something. But I didn't want *anything* between us. Besides," he chuckled softly, "it didn't seem quite right to go out to the car with the Indians just over the next ridge."

Casey felt her heart slide to the tip of her toes. Oh, God, she thought. Why does he have to be so damned honest? She gritted her teeth, trying to fight down a wave of agonizing jealousy. With eyes tightly closed she tried to reject the mental image of Dan holding another woman in his arms. Common sense told her he was a strong, virile man who would need an outlet for his passion and wouldn't have any trouble finding a woman to satisfy him. It was only natural he would be prepared in order to prevent any lasting entanglements.

"It isn't likely you've made me pregnant." Her voice was weakened by the depth of her emotion. "I'm due in a few days, so don't worry about it."

"Oh, God!" There was agony in his voice. "I didn't realize how that would sound to you. You think I carry something with me in case I can pick up a quick lay." His arms tightened around her and now she was the one to be cuddled and comforted. "I'll admit, sweetheart, that I'm far from being a monk, but I am more discriminating than that remark about contraceptives made me sound. The reason I have something with me now is that I knew if I got my hands on you I might not be able to stop and I wanted protection for you."

"You don't have to explain." Her words sounded like a sob of despair, much to her embarrassment. She tried to turn her face away when he lifted it, but his descending mouth was already on hers in a series of long, drugging kisses, and she surrendered to the inevitable flash of wildfire raging through her veins. Then it was over and he held her away so he could look into her eyes.

"Okay?" he whispered, his eyes searching hers.

"Okay."

There was an aching hunger in his kiss that effectively erased all thought of any predecessors. He gave her an affectionate squeeze and pressed her head to his shoulder.

"I think we had better start home tomorrow," he said quietly. "I've got to get back to the mill."

Casey ignored the first part of what he said. "The mill? What about your rugby team?"

"Oh, that. The season is over and I'm thinking very seriously about it being my last. I'll have more responsibilities now and won't want to be away from home for such long stretches."

"I'm sure your fans will be sorry to hear that."

"What about you? Are you sorry to hear about it, too?"

"What's it got to do with me? I never saw a rugby game in my life."

"It's got everything to do with you and you know it."

"Oh, Dan, I don't think . . ." She hesitated, not really knowing how to phrase what she wanted to say.

He ignored her words anyway. "Well? Don't you think we've vacationed long enough? We'll go by your apartment and pick up anything you want to take with you."

"I haven't said I'm going to Bend. I have plans for the next six months. Now that Judy has sublet my apartment I can afford to rent a place of my own."

"She didn't sublet it, sweetheart. I paid the rent for six months and you can repay me by house-sitting in Bend."

She tried to push herself away so she could see his face, but his hand on her head kept it firmly against his shoulder.

"Why did you tell me she had sublet it?" Her voice was almost angry.

"Think back, my Clementine. I told you it was taken care of. I didn't tell you it was sublet, but if you want to think of it as being sublet, you can." His voice took on a firm, positive tone. "I'm quite sure about how I feel and what I want. I want to marry you and live the rest of my life with you, but I don't want to rush *you* into anything. I want you to be absolutely sure you want me forever when we say our vows. So I'm giving us time to be together, to grow on each other. All I'm asking of you is to come with me to Bend, meet my family, and see the way I live. Then you can decide if you want to tie your life to mine. I don't think I'm asking too much of you."

Tears spilled from Casey's eyes. "Why are you like this? Why are you so good and sweet to me and I'm so bitchy? It's too onesided, Dan. I have nothing to offer you and you have everything to give to a woman. I don't even have a family back-ground with a positive approach to marriage. All the ones I've seen are nothing, a farce. I'm . . . I'm not even attractive anymore."

"You have yourself, Casey. Proud, independent, highly intelligent, and, as I'm discovering, sexy, loving, compassionate . . . and," she could feel the chuckle in his chest, "you're even beginning to believe we've been together in our other lives. So how can I not love my Guinevere, my Cleopatra, my Clementine?"

"And your Lucrezia Borgia?"

He hugged her tightly. "Even my Lucrezia Bor-gia, duchess of Ferrara, who did me in with a glass of poisoned wine."

"Oh, Dan. This can't last you know."

"It's lasted thousands of years," he laughed. "It'll last another forty or fifty."

Eight

Casey pulled out of the drive of the service station and onto the highway. She glanced in the rearview mirror at the big, blue car following her. It should have been comforting to know Dan was there behind her; instead she felt as if she were on a roller coaster and couldn't get off. He had packed the car, closed the cottage, and taken the key to the owner. He had even instructed the attendant at the station to check the oil and tires and to wash her windshield. When she had tried to pay for the gas and services he had shoved a credit card in the man's hand and she was ignored.

She should be grateful and flattered that he wanted to do these things for her. But in the light of day it all seemed strange and unreal. He was taking over her life so completely that when the letdown came, which it surely would, she wouldn't be able to handle it. What really frightened her now was the discovery that she possessed such a capacity for sensual pleasure. When her brief love

affairs had proved so unsatisfactory, she had sus-
pected she was a woman without much of a sex
drive, perhaps even frigid. It simply wasn't *her* to
respond to a man as she had responded to Dan,
all defenses down, without shame, without inhi-
bitions. She had surrendered that part of herself
she had always held back. Surrendered it willingly, joyfully. My God! Was this what it was like to
love someone? Was this the way her mother had
loved Eddie? God knew, she had seen the dangers
of that kind of physical attraction.

Casey looked down at the hands that gripped
the wheel. The crisscross of scars stood out prom-
inently despite the daily massage with creams.
This was reality. She had always taken pride in her
hands and nails; her fingers were long and slender, her nails perfectly formed. Now the thought
of sitting at a dinner table with friends or relatives of Dan's was unbearable. Why did she have
to think of such a stupid thing as that?

In that moment when she was lying beside Dan
she had foolishly agreed to go to Bend and meet
his family. It was crazy. Not because of her hands,
her scarred face, but because she was letting herself be drawn tighter and tighter into a trap that
would tear the heart out of her when she freed
herself from it. She was suddenly furious with
herself. Stupid, stupid! She wasn't ready for anything this heavy.

On the outskirts of Portland she pulled into the
parking lot of a fast food drive-in and Dan parked
beside her. Casey reached over and unlocked the
door on the passenger side of her car and Dan
opened it. She sat there looking at him. She didn't
say anything, because she was having trouble
breathing.

"What's the matter? Did the drive tire you out?"

A little to her surprise she found herself telling

him the truth, rather than her usual "No, I'm fine."

"I'm tired and . . . hungry, but that isn't why I stopped. I don't want to go with you to Bend." She thought, if I cry, I'll kill myself later on. I swear I will!

"I thought maybe you'd have second thoughts. It's all right, honey. Let's get something to eat and we can talk about it after." There was the click of the door as he pushed it shut.

Casey's heart was beating painfully fast and she had a knot of nausea in the pit of her stomach. *So he'd had second thoughts, too.* That was what she wanted, wasn't it? Then why did she feel like she'd been kicked in the stomach?

She sat in a booth while Dan went to the counter to order. Later he slid a tray containing three hamburgers, two large orders of french fries, and two malts on the table and sat down opposite her.

"This should tide us over for awhile."

His grin was so endearing, already so familiar, she could, do nothing but stare at him. Then to cover her confusion she began to eat as if she were starving, until the food backed up and refused to go down her throat. She carefully placed the half-eaten sandwich back in the Styrofoam box and picked up the malt. Her eyes roamed the room so she wouldn't have to look at Dan and locked with those of an attractive girl in another booth. The girl's eyes went to Dan and she said something to the woman beside her. Then they both began to scrutinize Casey and for the first time in years she cringed under a woman's stare. Casey looked away, but unerringly her eyes returned to the attractive girl who raised her brows in question when their eyes met. With insolent thoroughness, the girl surveyed Casey from head to toe, taking in the headscarf, the tremor in the scarred hand holding the malt cup, and Casey's stiff face.

A wave of savage resentment rose up in Casey. This was a sample of what she could expect as Dan's companion. Deliberately she smiled at him and held out her hand. He immediately covered it with his, but he didn't return her smile.

"What is it, sweetheart?"

She almost panicked. *My God! He reads me like a book.* She decided to be all up front, so she laughed lightly.

"There's a couple of women over there giving you the eye. I think they know you."

"The brunette with the frizzy hair?" He let his hand move over hers until he could clasp his fingers about her wrist. His eyes remained on Casey's face and she nodded. "They don't know me. They're just two women on the make. Ignore them."

"How do you know? They could be fans."

He shrugged his shoulders. "I doubt it. But if they have seen me play, so what?" He pushed a french fried potato in Casey's mouth, then filled his own. "Eat up, honey, so we can get going."

"I've had all I want."

"It's too bad we didn't stop at one of these places when we crossed the plains the first time." His dark eyes were mischievous.

"We did stop. Remember? We had a sourdough biscuit and a slab of side pork." She heard her own giggle with a feeling of wonder.

"Oh, yes. I remember, now. We made love in the back of the wagon and the train went off without us."

Casey forgot the women across the room, forgot her determination to keep her independence, forgot everything as she gazed into warm, smiling gray-black eyes. But she remembered when she was alone in her car on the way to her apartment and she began to outline arguments for not going to Bend.

Dan parked behind her and they walked into the building together. He produced a key and opened the door of her apartment as if he lived there—which, she supposed, he did, as long as he paid the rent.

"Run along and take a bath and get on something comfortable," he said and took the scarf from her head. "I've got some calls to make. Call me and I'll come and wash your back." He patted her affectionately on the bottom.

The gesture angered her. "Dammit! Stop treating me like I was a child," she almost shouted, her golden eyes sparkling. She was amazed at the range of emotions he could arouse in her.

"Don't swear," he said calmly.

"I'll swear any *damn* time I please!"

"Act like a child and you'll be treated like one."

His rational calmness was irritating and she flounced into the bathroom. His chuckle did nothing to douse the blaze of resentment that burned through her because she knew he only had to touch her, caress her, and she would melt like an ice cream cone on a hot day. She shut the door and locked it, more determined than ever to end the relationship before he discovered he could reduce her to a mass of quivering jelly.

While she showered all sorts of wild thoughts floated through her mind. She'd slick her hair back in a ponytail and wear that sleeveless, almost frontless, sundress she'd made last summer . . . and an earring on her good ear. She'd let him see her scars—and if that didn't put him off, nothing would! She had acted like a sex-starved female, she fumed. Was it something basic to her character that was touched by his overwhelming virility? Or was it because she had been starved for years, hungry for love and attention, waiting to be wanted, reaching for what she thought was real at last? Dan had given her a taste of what she had been denied and she had eagerly grabbed it.

"Oh, God! I'm nothing, but chicken," she muttered aloud when she dried her hair and arranged it about her face. "Admit it, Casey, you stupid creature—you'd rather die than go out there and face him in a sundress with your hair in a ponytail!"

When she finally walked into the small living room in velour pants and shirt, she felt confident that she looked as attractive as she possibly could. She needed that confidence. Dan had made coffee and brought the pot and cups to the table beside the couch. She felt a tremor in her heart when he looked up and smiled.

"Coffee?"

"Sure."

"You look good enough to eat."

Casey raised her brows. "I never cared for prunes, myself." He chuckled at her self-directed sarcasm, accepting it as an apology. She decided her best plan was attack, putting him on the defensive for a change. She accepted the cup he handed to her and went to sit on the recliner, propping her feet up on the footstool. Somehow it seemed there was more of a barrier between them. "I'm not going to Bend with you. I'll give you a check for the money you paid my landlord." She stated the facts calmly and was rather proud of the steadiness of her voice.

"What are you afraid of?" He reached down and removed his shoes and stretched his legs out in front of him as if he didn't have a care in the world.

"I'm not afraid of anything. Why should I be? I like my life the way it is." She set the cup down on the table so he wouldn't see her hands trembling.

"Yes, you are. You're afraid of commitment.

You're afraid of marriage. You're afraid you can't handle it."

"I'm not afraid of it," she said heatedly. "I just want no part of it. Marital fidelity isn't possible in this age of sexual freedom and I'll not enter into a marriage that has only half a chance of lasting."

"I disagree. One man and one woman can stay happily married forever, but they have to *want* to stay married. Ecstasy and monogamy are not mutually exclusive," he said politely, almost daring her to object.

"Where have you been for the last few years? Statistics tell us that husbands and *wives* are turning with increasing frequency to new partners. Two thirds of all married men have extramarital affairs. It seems stupid to me that people get married in the first place."

He grinned. "Do you want to live with me in sin?"

"I don't want to live with you at all," she snapped. "I'm trying to explain why I don't want this relationship to go any farther."

"You think I'll run out on you like Ed Farrow did your mother." He wasn't smiling, now. "You know, Casey, sometimes scars that *don't* show are the worst."

Casey froze. "You're saying that what my father did warped my thinking?"

"It's bound to have," he said quietly.

"Well maybe it has, but it taught me one thing. Depend on yourself. If you let yourself down you can't blame someone else." Casey fumed inwardly. Why couldn't she think of all the clever things she'd thought of to say when she was in the car?

"I think you've got the cart before the horse, my Clementine. I haven't actually asked you to marry me . . . yet."

Casey almost gasped with embarrassment. She

could feel the blood rush to her face and then she looked at him. He was grinning broadly and his eyes were glittering devilishly. She prayed for the strength to throw her cup at him. Suddenly he sat up straight and planted his stockinged feet flat on the floor.

"If you want statistics, love, I can give you a few. The majority of marriages break up because of . . . boredom. The wife is bored with the husband or it's the other way around. There's no danger of that happening to us. We can always get back on the wagon train or float down the Nile."

She pressed her lips together, didn't answer, and the silence dragged. Then she looked at him and he winked at her. She couldn't keep the corners of her mouth from turning up.

"Damn you, Dan. This is a serious conversation!"

"Sure it is, sweetheart." He was on his feet and pulling her off the recliner. "It's so serious, it's tired me out and I need a nap. I didn't get much sleep last night and it was all your fault." He sank down on the couch taking her with him. "After our nap we'll have another serious talk." He pressed his back against the couch and pulled her back tightly to his chest. "Does that hurt your ear? No? Then go to sleep," he commanded gently and buried his nose and his lips in her hair.

It hadn't occurred to Casey to resist the pull of his arms. Her mind and her body were tired and it was comforting to be held. Her buttocks pressed against the front of his jeans and his knees pressed the back of hers. She could feel the steady beat of his heart against her back and she wondered for the hundredth time about the fate that had brought this man to her on that foggy night.

That evening when Dan asked if she wanted to go out to eat, Casey shook her head vigorously.

"I have some canned soup and a few other things I keep in stock if you think you can survive on a skimpy meal."

"I'm not fussy. Heat it up while I unload your car and park it. You can drive mine when we get to Bend."

"Dan, I'll drive my own car."

"That's foolish. I've got two more cars at home." He opened her purse and took out her keys.

"I don't understand you. I said—"

"Good!" He cut off her words with the quick pressure of his mouth. "If you don't understand me, you won't be bored and we won't end up one of those statistics you were telling me about."

Casey thought surely he would make a negative comment when she got out her portable sewing machine, a large box of fabric she had bought at various times when they were on sale, patterns, and miscellaneous sewing items. But he merely peeked into the box, lifted out a piece of knit material with large wine-red and blue stripes and held it up to him.

"Would this make a shirt?"

"No!" Casey laughed and took it from him and stuffed it back in the box. "You'd look like the barrel they race around at the rodeo!"

"Yeah?" He dropped down beside her on the floor. "What's in there you could make into a shirt for me?"

"You're not kidding? You'd wear a shirt I made?"

"I said I would. Don't you believe anything I say?" He pounced on her and pushed her gently down on the carpet. "I'll probably have a hernia by the time I load all your stuff in the car, but I'm willing to risk it for a shirt . . . and a kiss." He leaned over her, holding her wrist lightly. She tried to free her hand to be sure her hair still covered her ear, but he refused to release it, so she turned her head to one side. "It's been hours since I've kissed my Guinevere," he said huskily. "I don't count those little pecks you gave me." He kissed her long, his mouth wonderfully warm and passionate. "Everything about you turns me on. That short upper lip." He stroked it with his tongue. "This little crease beside your mouth." He licked it. "You've got beautiful thick eyelashes. And right here at the corners of your eyes you're going to have little smile lines." His lips touched each eye. "You're going to get more and more beautiful as you grow older."

"Don't—"

"Hush. I know you don't want me to say you're beautiful, but I will say it, my beautiful Guinevere—Cleopatra—Clementine. Put your arms around your lord and master." He lifted her arms to encircle his neck.

"Lord and master? Ha! I find you maddening, puzzling, a real chauvinist! The hair on your chest tickles me and the whiskers on your chin scratch me." Her fingers reached inside his shirt and she gave a hard yank to a thick tuff of hair, then tried to roll away when he yelped.

He growled fiercely and his long arms locked her to him and they rolled on the floor. Casey heard her own peals of laughter, disbelieving they were her own. This lightheartedness wasn't real. This wasn't . . . *her,* but, oh, how wonderful to be in his arms playing like two teenagers. Dan rolled her over him and they came up against the couch. He locked her to the floor with his arms and legs and laughed down into her smiling eyes.

"I'm going to have to teach you some respect for your lord." He drew his brows together in a heavy frown. "That is, if I have the strength after I make wild, passionate love to you." He made a sound deep in his throat like an aroused tom cat and she couldn't suppress her laughter.

"I must warn you. I've had a course in jujitsu and you are leaving a most vulnerable spot unprotected." She giggled in delight at his evident surprise.

"You mean you'd . . .?"

"Uh-huh." Her laughing eyes were glittering pools of molten gold.

"You'd hamper our . . . love life?"

"Uh-huh."

A little to her surprise, he pulled his upper body away from her, but nestled that *vulnerable* part of him tight against her thigh. He looked past her face and focused his eyes on the carpet.

"What a cold, hard lady. I can't believe that she would injure my delicate parts. She's more Lucrezia than Guinevere, more Lizzie Borden than Clementine!" His conversational tone was addressed to thin air. "She pulls the hair on my chest, calls me a chauvinist, tells me I'm maddening."

Casey reached up and enclosed his face with her palms. "Ahhh . . . poor baby." She had never felt so good, so free, so happy. "I'll kiss it and make it better." This childish play had unleashed the reserve she normally kept under such tight control.

"It'll take more than one," he said sulkily.

"I think I can manage." She circled his neck with her arms and pulled his head down to hers. With her lips tightly puckered she made loud smacking sounds against his lips. Then laughter bubbled up and out of her throat.

He gazed into her laughing eyes and shook his head. Then lightning fast his fingers found her ribs and raked across them. She tried to knock his hands away, but he was pressing her to the floor. Peals of laughter rang out.

"Don't! Don't! Oh, please, Dan. I can't stand to be tickled. Stop! Stop! Or . . . I'll have an accident!"

He stopped immediately and grinned down at her. "You'll what?"

"Have an . . . an accident, you big brute!"

It was his turn to roar with laughter. "You mean you'd—"

Her hand came up and covered his mouth and he nipped at her fingers. Then he rolled over on his back, taking her with him. The enchantment grew in the circle of Dan's arms. She didn't speak, finding words an inadequate means of expressing her feelings. Never had she felt this light, this carefree, this close to another human being. When he turned so his lips could reach hers, she welcomed them gladly.

Closing her eyes, Casey savored the sweet ecstasy his mouth created with its warm exploration of hers and returned the pressure, the nibbling, giving as much as she was receiving. He raised his head and she looked into dark smoldering eyes.

"I want you for my wife, my partner, my lover." There was a ragged edge to his voice, a roughness to his breathing. It echoed much of what Casey was feeling until his hand slid beneath her shirt and began to pull it up over her breast. She caught his wrist.

"Please, don't." Her voice was a whispered plea.

"Sweetheart . . . why? I know you want me to love you. I can tell by the beat of your heart, by the movements your hips are making against mine."

"Not here," she whispered anxiously.

"Love doesn't always have to be in the bed in the dark," he insisted. She turned her face away, but he saw the glimmer of tears. "But if that's the way m'lady wants it to be. . . . Sweetheart, look at me. You do like being my lady?"

"You know I do," she said softly and wound her

arms about his neck. She kissed his ear, his cheek, ran her fingers through his springy black hair.

"We'll play it your way for awhile, sweetheart. You'll get over your shyness with me." He got to his feet and pulled her up beside him. "Sleepy?"

"No, but I can't wait to go to bed."

"Mmmmm . . . best offer I've had all day. I left this number for my brother to call. I think I'll call him because I have a feeling I won't want to be disturbed later on." He kissed her nose and pushed her gently toward the bedroom door.

The rain was pouring down by the time they reached the outskirts of Portland. Casey was glad now that she wasn't driving. Something about the gray day and the sheets of rain hitting the windshield reminded her of that foggy night on the highway.

Dan's hand left the wheel and reached for her arm. "Come closer."

She went willingly, her shoulder tucked behind his, her hip and thigh in contact with his. He was an excellent driver and kept his eyes straight ahead.

"I like you close." He said the words simply.

She placed her hand on his thigh and his hand immediately dropped to cover it. Being with Dan was like a dream. Maybe that was what bothered her. Dreams seldom came true. She looked at his profile; concentration furrowed his brow. He took driving seriously. I love you, Lancelot, she told him silently. I don't want you to be a dream. I want all of this to be real. And maybe, just maybe . . .

"Maybe your father will pay us a visit." Dan's voice broke into her thoughts.

"I doubt it. He always wants to know where I am. That's why I called him. I think he suffers a guilt complex, but he wouldn't know a guilt feeling if it jumped up and bit him." After a while she added, "I left a note for Judy. She would be the one to miss me."

"Only Judy?"

"The rest of my friends were connected with my job and I don't think I'll be seeing much of them."

"Who needs friends like that?" His voice sounded cold for a minute.

Casey leaned her cheek against his shoulder. "Tell me about Bend. Is your mother at home now?"

"She's in New York with one of her sisters. My mother has a passion for plays. She's been addicted to them for as long as I can remember. She and my aunt take in every play on Broadway and then go to London to see some more."

"London? To see a play?"

"Well, not just to see plays. She has friends there. Aunt Bea is the exact opposite of my mother and her other sister. She lives right across the fence from us and you couldn't get her out of Oregon with a team of mules." Casey could tell from the amusement and affection that colored his tone of voice that he liked his Aunt Bea.

"Will I be seeing her?"

"You bet." He took his eyes from the road long enough to grin at her. "Aunt Bea is quite a woman. She's an apiarist."

"Your aunt is a beekeeper?"

"Ironic, isn't it? My aunt Bea, the beekeeper. She's had bees for the last thirty years. Her yard is surrounded with hives and honey houses. She sells honey to all the local markets and to some stores in Portland. 'Aunt Bea's Honey.' She's even got her picture on the label."

"You're kidding."

Dan laughed. "I'm not kidding. She had a picture of a honey bee drawn with her head on the body. Appropriate, don't you think?"

"Well . . . uh, no doubt about that. Is she married?"

"Her husband died about twenty years ago. She has no children of her own, but she claims me. She's anxious to meet you and will probably give you the third degree."

"Why would she do that? And how does she know about me?" Casey suddenly was nervous and her words came out sharp and staccato.

"She's anxious to know you because she loves me and will want to check you out to be sure you're everything I told her you were." He put his hand on the inside of her thigh and pressed her leg to his.

"Dan! You didn't tell your family there was any-thing . . . ah . . . personal between us?" She practically groaned.

"Of course I did. I told them I wanted to marry you. Why shouldn't I tell them?" He sounded proud.

"Because . . . we haven't decided anything for sure."

"I have. If you turn me down you'll embarrass me and I'll lose credibility with my family."

"I never know when you're teasing. You *are* teasing?" She looked horrified. "I thought I was going to house-sit, not be put on display so your family can decide if I'm good enough." Taut nerves had put an even sharper edge to her voice.

"I was teasing. You'll love Aunt Bea and she'll love you. The first thing she'll do is bring you a cookbook that substitutes honey for sugar in all the recipes. Then she'll give you a lecture on health food." He chuckled. "I imagine you can tell her a thing or two about that."

"Where do *you* live?" The thought had just oc-curred to her.

"There's a cabin out at the mill. I stay there sometimes. Sometimes I stay at the house. My dog is at the house and I have to see her." He braked to allow a car to pass and squeeze in ahead of them. "Damn fool! Sometimes I think they should give I.Q. and sanity tests before they give out driver's licences."

"Who's taking care of the house now?" Casey asked quietly. It was slowly dawning upon her that the house-sitting job was a ruse to get her to Bend.

"Aunt Bea, part of the time, and me, part of the time. The rest of the time my sisters-in-law come out. Mom has a million plants in the house."

"I love house plants," she said lamely and lapsed into silence.

The country they passed through was beautiful. The highway went through Mt. Hood National Forest and across the Warm Springs Indian Reservation. They turned south at a town called Madras.

"It won't be long now," Dan said. "We have several wilderness areas near by. Some day we'll go backpacking." He seemed to sense her nervousness and talked on calmly about the landmarks they passed. "We're not too far from Bachelor Mountain. A friend of mine has a year-round lodge up there. It's a skier's dream. The snow is dry and the temperature perfect. Do you ski?"

"A little. I'm not an expert, by any means."

"They have runs for every ability level." He was holding her hand tightly. It was as if he was trying to give her strength for something that would be difficult for her. They didn't talk until they drove into Bend. "It's not much compared to Portland." He laughed, lightly. It was a proud laugh, in no way apologetic. "This is our main street." Casey thought the town was charming. It looked like a small thriving community. Most of the parking places were full. They passed quickly through town and out onto the highway again. "We live out of town along the Deschutes River. We're almost home, sweetheart."

Casey gently tugged her hand loose from Dan's and adjusted the scarf over her ears.

Nine

Dan turned the car onto a narrow blacktopped road which cut a swath through tall, dark cedar trees. Eventually the woods thinned out and they drove past a fenced meadow where a bay mare and colt grazed. The colt came trotting inquisitively to the fence and watched them pass, then kicked up its heels and went back to its mother. They drove through another wooded area and the trees gave way suddenly to a view of lawns sweeping up to the front of a large brown-shingled house. Dan turned up a narrow lane flanked with bushes and onto a wide flagged drive.

Casey felt a flutter of relief. Somehow she had imagined a flock of Dan's relatives would be waiting outside the house and she would have to run the gamut of appraising eyes. The double-hatched front door, with strap hinges of a trefoil pattern, were closed. The hip-roofed house, sides and roof, was covered with weathered shingles and looked settled, completely at ease in its surroundings.

There was a drive that circled around to garages attached to the side of the house, but Dan stopped the car near the front door.

Casey turned solemn eyes to him. "It's lovely. It looks so calm and peaceful."

Dan squeezed her hand. "Somehow I knew you'd like it. C'mon. The sun came out to welcome you to your new home." He got out of the car and waited for her to slide under the wheel.

Inside the house he turned her toward the big living room, which ran across the entire front of the house, leading into a dining ell. It was a fireplace, leather, and chintz room, with large soft couches and chairs and colonial-type curtains. A stately grandfather clock presided by the staircase opposite the front door. The broad-planked floors that gleamed beneath braided wool rugs told her the house was old and rooms had probably been added from time to time. The house seemed exactly right for Dan now that she saw him here. It reflected comfort, taste, and warm serenity.

He led her into a large, windowed kitchen, scrupulously clean and shining. Plants lined wide window ledges and brass cookware hung over the island counter stove. A round oak table and high-backed chairs sat at one end with a view of the river beyond. The table was set with quilted print placemats and crockery. A fresh-baked pie sat on the counter. From the kitchen you stepped out on a screened porch, which looked as if it ran the length of the house.

Dan hadn't spoken a word while he led her through the house. Now he came to her and put his arms around her and kissed her with an aching hunger. "I want to show you the upstairs."

He took her hand and they went back to the entry and up half a dozen steps to a landing where the steps turned at right angles for the longer portion of the rise. The door to the first room stood invitingly open and sun shone onto the light tan carpet from the dormer windows. There was a large bed with heavy, carved walnut posts and a woven spread of muted blues, reds, and off-white. It was a masculine room, from the heavy dark furniture to the comfortable leather chairs. There were two doors on the right wall. One led to a walk-in closet and the other to a bathroom. The room looked and smelled like Dan.

"Yours?" Casey spoke for the first time since she entered the house.

"Ours?" It was a question.

Casey looked deeply into his quiet dark eyes and slowly shook her head.

"I'll wear out the hall carpet," he muttered menacingly.

Casey thought silence the best reproof, and allowed him to usher her, with his hand in the center of her back, down the hall to another room.

"There are four bedrooms up here and a small apartment over the garage. We used to have live-in help." Dan indicated the door opposite his room. "That one's my mother's, although she's seldom here. The next room is small, but I thought it might do for a sewing room," he announced smoothly. "This room can be yours until we are married, as long as you won't share mine." He opened a door and stepped aside for her to enter.

The room was large and square and was set in the corner of the house. The walls were white, the carpet emerald green, the chairs and tables white wicker. The queen-sized bed had a bookcase headboard and was covered with an Indian-print spread in a pattern that matched the cushions on the chairs and the low couch. Large floor vases were filled with fragrant flowers. It was so different from the rest of the house that she had to keep her face from showing her surprise, especially since Dan was watching her and his eyes were dancing with mischief.

"Aunt Bea decided this room needed an overhaul a few years ago. She said it looked like a morgue. This is the result."

"It's lovely, and it certainly doesn't resemble a morgue now."

Casey smiled at him and he pulled her into his arms. She leaned compliantly against him and he stroked her face lovingly with his fingertips.

"I like seeing you in my house."

"I thought it was your mother's house."

"Don't get technical," he scolded. His face was very stern, but his eyes were teasing and his fingers trailed down her neck, tracing the outline of her shoulder before moving, ever so delicately, to her breast.

"Dan Murdock, you're a con artist, a lecher, an oversexed jerk, cad, louse . . . but I . . ."

"But you what, my Juliet?" His chuckle rumbled in his chest.

"But nothing, my Romeo. Kiss me so I can go forth to procure yon raiment and return thus to this gallery."

He groaned. "You just blew it. You'd make a lousy Juliet."

"Oh, you think so!" Her fingers dug into his ribs and she planted her feet on top his loafers. Holding both of her arms to her sides he lifted her off her feet.

"You know what you're asking for?"

"You better not!" she gasped. "You know what'll happen."

"You'll have an accident?"

"Right!"

"I'd rather do this anyway." He set her on her feet and lifted her arms to encircle his neck. "Mmmmm . . ." he said when he lifted his mouth from hers, "you taste like apple pie."

"You've got your mind on what's sitting on the counter downstairs," she said softly against his lips.

"Wrong. My mind's not on my stomach at all. It's on yours." He kissed her, softly at first, and then harder, his arms holding her close, his mouth clamped tightly to hers.

She melted into his kiss. She couldn't have resisted if she had wanted to, but she didn't want to. She just wanted to be there, next to him, feeling the warmth of his skin and the strength of his arms, and smelling the scent of him that was so familiar to her. He lifted his mouth. His eyes were very close. She could see her reflection in them.

"I love you Cassandra. That's all. I just love you. No demands, no promises asked."

"It's crazy. But I think I love you, too, Lancelot." She said it with a soft smile and a mist in her eyes. *Think?* Forgive me, darling, for not saying it more convincingly, she told him silently. But I've got to leave some room to maneuver.

"Ya-hooo . . . Daniel. I've been waiting down here for a long time. Are you up there smooching with that girl?"

"Aunt Bea," Dan whispered. "She's very earthy. I'm surprised she didn't come on up in hopes of catching us in bed."

Casey smiled broadly. "I haven't heard 'smooching' for ages."

"She's a very liberated woman."

"The birds and the bees and all that?"

"She's straitlaced about a lot of things. Her most endearing quality is that you always know where you stand with Aunt Bea. C'mon, and meet her." Sensing her sudden anxiety about measuring up to someone he obviously cared for, he flung his arm around her shoulder. "She's been after me for years to marry some 'nice girl.' She'll have you involved with her honey business before you know it."

The woman waiting at the bottom of the steps had short, gray hair, large, wide-spaced eyes, and a broad smile. She was wearing jeans and a T-shirt that said AUNT BEA IS A HONEY.

Dan greeted her with a kiss on the cheek, bending low because her head barely came to his armpit. She made up for her lack of height with a generously rounded bosom and tummy.

"Hi, Aunt Bea. This is Cassandra Farrow, but call her Casey."

"Hello, Casey." She held out her hand. There was nothing but surprise and pleasure in her broad smile. Her grip was warm and strong and her dark eyes twinkled up at Dan. "My, my. Isn't she nice and tall? And her hair and eyes are like . . . honey."

"I knew you'd say that." Dan's voice was resigned, but amused.

"Why'd you wait so long to bring her home?"

"I was working on it as fast as I could, Aunt Honey Bea."

Aunt Bea nodded with satisfaction. Casey glanced at Dan and could tell that he was pleased with the warm reception his aunt had given her.

"Let's have some coffee, Casey, and get acquainted. Daniel has a woman friend out back that's having a fit because he hasn't been out to see her." Aunt Bea's eyes took on the same gleam as Dan's when he was teasing. "Her name's Sadie and she's got the most gorgeous blue eyes you ever saw."

Casey walked beside the small woman. Dan followed.

"We don't want to keep him from his adoring public," Casey said confidentially to Aunt Bea and reached back to slap Dan's hand away after his fingers nipped her buttock.

Minutes later Dan opened the porch door and a large, black and brown dog walked sedately into the kitchen. It stopped several feet from where Casey sat at the round table and tilted its head inquiringly. Aunt Bea was right about the eyes. They were a startling blue in the dog's dark face.

"Sit and say hello to Casey, Sadie," Dan commanded firmly.

Sadie backed up a few steps and sat down, lifted her nose to the ceiling, and let out a mournful howl. She looked at Dan, then repeated the greeting even louder and longer.

"And hello to you, too," Casey said and patted her thigh. The dog came to her and laid her jowls on her lap, her eyes never leaving Casey's face. "What kind of dog is she?" Casey lifted her hand and gently stroked the massive head.

"Siberian Husky. Her name is Sovetskaya, but we call her Sadie."

"I can understand why."

Aunt Bea brought the coffee pot to the table and set it on a tile trivit. "Are you having coffee with us, Daniel?"

"Sure, if I can have some pie to go with it. Then I'll unload the car."

"Marge called this morning. The thundering herd will be here this evening. She said she and Helen will go by the fried chicken place and bring out a couple of tubs of chicken and they'll get potato salad from the deli. You're to start up the charcoal burner because some of the kids will want hot-dogs."

"Okay." Dan pulled out a chair and sat down with his back to the windows. "How about Fred and Hank? Are they going to tear themselves away from the mill?"

"Are you kidding? Wild horses couldn't keep them away." Aunt Bea chuckled. "They can't wait to meet Casey."

Casey's stomach began to churn and, as she was inclined to do when she became nervous, she tugged the scarf down more securely over her ears. Dan was watching her and the tender regard in his eyes made her hand tremble when she reached for her coffee cup. At that moment she glanced at Aunt Bea who was looking intently at the scarred hand they lay on the table. Automatically Casey drew it down onto her lap.

"The family, all at once, is a pretty big dose for you, sweetheart. Think you're up to it?"

Casey didn't dare look at Aunt Bea. Dan's use of the endearment would certainly put their relationship on an intimate level. There was no use pretending she had come here to house-sit. Dan had brought her here for his family's approval and the big test would be tonight. Dear Lord! She'd had no experience in integrating into a family structure, especially one as close-knit as this one. She looked at Dan with almost unseeing eyes as she struggled with her inner conflict.

She still hadn't answered Dan's question when the phone rang and he went to the other end of the kitchen to answer it. Casey felt the feathery touch of his fingers on her neck when he passed her and sudden tears ached behind eyes that were drawn to Aunt Bea to see her reaction to Dan's caress.

"I never thought I'd see the day." There was a happy smile on the softly wrinkled face and her eyes shone like twin stars. "Daniel's head over heels in love with you, isn't he? I knew that if he ever found the right woman he would be just like his father and the boys. The men in this family choose a wife carefully then love her to distraction. Of course, we were all worried there for awhile. What with all the women hot for him because he was a rugby player and all. But I told

Hank and Fred, give him some rope and he'll sort them all out and find the right girl."

Casey looked at her for a long time before she said, "How do you know I'm the right girl? You know nothing about me and I could be just another one of the groupies as far as you know."

"I haven't lived all these fifty-five years under a rock. If you'd been one of *them*, Daniel wouldn't have had to tell you this was his mother's house and that you were coming to house-sit." Aunt Bea delivered the statement positively.

Casey looked at her in wide-eyed amazement, but before she could form a reply Dan came back to the table.

"Hank said I may have to be gone for several days at the end of the week. I'm glad the family is coming over so you can get acquainted. They'll keep you company while I'm gone."

"I'll have plenty to keep me busy. I've got my sewing, you know."

They ate large slices of fresh apple pie and talked about sewing. Aunt Bea was so comfortable to be with that Casey almost forgot the ordeal waiting for her at the end of the day.

"More pie, Daniel? I baked it before I knew about the clan gathering. I've more in the freezer I'll bake this afternoon. Do you think four will be enough?"

"Four pies?" Casey asked with disbelief.

Dan laughed. "There are twelve kids and seven grown-ups. Nineteen of us, counting you, sweetheart."

"Lucy and Maryann are coming with Helen," Aunt Bea said flatly and Casey darted a glance at her.

"Is she back?" Dan raised his brows, then grinned at Casey. "Helen's sister. That'll make twenty-one. Better put in another pie, Aunt Bea."

The afternoon flew by. Aunt Bea went back

through the break in the fence to her own home to put the pies in the oven. Dan unloaded the car and helped Casey put her things away. His obvious pleasure at having her here was the only thing that kept panic at bay. Casey went over in her mind, time and again, what she would wear this evening and how she would fix her hair. It was almost as if she were a schoolgirl again going to her first prom. It brought home to her just how much her self-confidence had slipped since the accident.

She showered, washed her hair, blew it dry, and turned it toward her face with the curling iron. She was quite pleased with the result. But what to wear? She was standing in the closet going through her choices when Dan tapped on the door and came into the room. He came up behind her and wrapped his arms around her. She could feel the hardness of his body through the heavy robe she was wearing.

"You smell good." His nose nuzzled her neck. "I came to tell you to wear something old. The kids will want a baseball game."

"Dan . . ." She turned in his arms. "I should punch you in the nose for putting me through this." The last of her words came out in a shaken whisper because his lips were tormenting hers. Her arms went up and around his neck and the familiar excitement began to throb through her body. Holding her nose to his face so she could smell the scents of his skin and hair, she let her fingers curl into the damp crispness at the back of his head.

"What are you worrying about? You're not shy? Anyone that can give a demonstration before several hundred people can surely handle twenty people, most of them kids."

"That was different. Dan . . . this is all too new. I wish I hadn't come. I know they'll think that we're sleeping together and that I've latched on to you since the accident. I don't like this feeling of being a hanger on'er," she ended breathlessly.

"If that isn't the craziest thing I ever heard," he chided gently. "Do you think I need my big brothers' approval before I select the woman I'm going to live with for the rest of my life? I want them to like you and you to like them, but if that doesn't happen it won't make the slightest difference. It's your approval I want, my Guinevere."

Casey was only half aware of what he was saying. She leaned against him and he bent his head, hesitating for an unbearable moment before touching her lips. All the emotional bruising melted and flowed from under the balm of his lips. Her mouth clung to his for a moment of incredible sweetness.

Very softly she said, "I'm scared."

"You needn't be scared of anything. I'll be beside you." He kissed her several times in quick succession. "Feel better?"

She nodded and looked deeply into the serious dark eyes that could sparkle with anger or amusement. "I'll make out."

"Tomorrow is a school day so they won't stay late. Now get on some jeans and a sweater. It's cold here when the sun goes down." His hands went to the belt of her robe. "I'll stay and help you," he said with his best villainous leer.

"Get out of here, Daniel, or I'll scream for Aunt Bea," she threatened softly.

"Smart-ass brat! We'll take up where we left off when we get rid of the thundering herd, as Aunt Bea calls them." He kissed her again as if to set a seal on his promise.

When Casey went downstairs she was wearing a bulky, soft knit sweater, jeans, and sandals. The gold sweater hugged her slim hips and was held close by a wide leather belt. She carried a silk scarf to hold her hair in place when she went outside. When she went into the kitchen, Dan was tearing the plastic wrap off a large stack of paper plates. He looked at her and let the wrap slide to the floor. Silently he opened his arms and she walked into them.

"You look as sweet and soft as a toasted marshmallow, all gold and white and delicious. Give me a kiss, then help me get this stuff out to the table on the porch. I think they'll be too many bugs for us to eat outside tonight."

Casey covered the two long picnic tables with a terry cloth cover and they set cups, plates, napkins, and silver on one end.

"Is this all we have to do?"

"We'll make coffee later. We've got a good thirty minutes before they descend on us and I want to spend it quietly with you." He took her hand and they walked slowly through the kitchen and into the living room.

There was a fragile magic around them. They were in perfect harmony. It was as if they had always been together, Casey thought as she looked at his tousled hair, nose leaning to one side. He wasn't handsome, certainly; he didn't have to be, with those compelling eyes and perfect body. Even in jeans and sweat shirt he looked like the commercial for a body building ad.

He tugged on her hand and they sank down on the couch. He gathered her in his arms, and pressed his face into her hair, being careful not to muss it, as if knowing how important it was to her to have it carefully arranged.

"Dan . . . how did you manage to stay single for so long?"

"I almost married once, but as the time drew closer to take the fatal plunge I knew that things weren't right. I used a delaying tactic and, sure enough, she backed out when she found out I was just a working stiff like the rest of the people in our company." A small smile played at the corners of his mouth as he watched her reaction through half closed lids.

"You don't seem to be exactly poor? Were you heartbroken?"

"Oh, God love you. You haven't a clue to what some women are like, have you?" He was amused and laughter rippled in his voice as he rocked her back and forth in his arms. "To someone whose papa could back a movie she wanted to be in and furnish her with her own Lear Jet, I was poor. Then, when she found out I had no intention of joining her and living off papa, she decided she didn't love me after all. All this happened when I was young and going over *fool's hill.*"

"Fool's hill? What's that?"

"That's the time in your life when you think the world's your oyster and you do dumb things." He looked into her eyes, rubbed her nose with his. His eyes were dancing with devilment and the slight upturning smile of his lips was boyish. "You took a lot of time with your makeup tonight. You *are* beautiful. Hush!" He put his fingers over her lips when she closed them firmly. "I've only seen pictures of you *without* the scar. I couldn't love you more if it wasn't there." Gentle fingers traced the outline of the scar and for the first time they touched the mangled ear beneath her hair.

Casey froze. Then he was kissing her, starting out with a sort of apologetic pressure of lips on hers, but the gentleness gave way to mutual need for a more satisfying kiss. His fingers fumbled with the belt at her waist, loosened it, and burrowed beneath the sweater to her breast. She had lost her fear that his hand would find its way to the breast that was injured. Not since that first time had he attempted to touch it.

Casey's makeup was being spoiled. She could

have pulled away, but she didn't. It was reckless and idiotic to make love here on the couch, but it was earthshaking the way his mouth moved lazily, sensually, teasing and playing with hers. Her hand slid under his shirt and flattened on his chest. The rough texture of the hair on his chest always excited her as did the smooth flesh over his ribs. He worked at the zipper on her jeans.

"Oh, Dan . . . we can't!"

"Why can't we? No one will come but Aunt Bea."

"No one but Aunt Bea! Oh, Dan, you idiot!"

His kiss deepened to hot drugging sweetness and she was floating on air. Her hands slipped inside his pants, inside the cotton briefs, and she heard the low rumble in his throat.

The back door banged. "Ya-hooo! Daniel! I need some help getting the pies over."

The language Dan used as Casey hastily withdrew her hands caused a giggle to burst from her lips.

"Remind me to put a lock on that damn door," he growled. Then, "Oh, God!"

Casey's eyes followed his to where the zipper on his fly was in danger of bursting. She couldn't stop her peal of laughter. She fastened her belt and tossed the newspaper over his lap.

"Read the paper. I'll help Aunt Bea. Big Dan Murdock, helpless as a baby," she taunted.

"Depraved hussy," he called softly as she left the room.

Casey couldn't imagine how Aunt Bea got through the screen door with a pie in each hand, but she had managed.

"You two been smoochin' again? Daniel's kissed all your lip rouge off. I'll swear. That boy won't give you any rest till you marry him, and not then for awhile. He'll probably keep you in bed for a week. That's what his pa did to his ma. She was pregnant with Hank before she got out of bed."

The plain talk brought color to Casey's cheeks. "Ah . . . Mrs. . . . Dan never did tell me your name."

"Yes, he did. Aunt Bea's my name." Dark eyes smiled up at Casey and a plump arm circled her waist. "Don't be afraid you're getting too familiar. Everybody calls me Aunt Bea."

"Then I will, too. I was already thinking of you as Aunt Bea."

"I suppose you two are conspiring against me." Dan's voice came from behind them.

Casey looked back, eyes wide, and asked innocently, "Did you get the paper read . . . already?"

He cupped her buttock with a strong hand. "Yes, I got the paper read . . . already," he mimicked. "Do you want me to run over and get the rest of the pies, Aunt Bea?"

"I'll go with you. Casey needs to go upstairs and put on more lip rouge. Then you leave her be, Daniel. She wants to look nice tonight."

Casey moved her hand to pat Dan's cheek, smiling wickedly at him. "Mind what your Aunt Bea tells you," she cautioned and scurried out of his reach.

Ten

Casey was alone in the kitchen with Aunt Bea when she heard the dog bark, then a car door slam. Soon the sound of a woman's voice giving orders with the precision of a drill sergeant reached her ears.

"John take this carton of chicken to the kitchen. Don't go through the house, Jim. Julie take the baby's hand and both of you stay away from Sadie. Don't rush off, Justin. We've more things to carry in."

Casey sank down on a stool because she couldn't have stood a second longer. Her legs were trembling. *Smile, Casey.* Put that smile on automatic. Don't let anyone know what's really going on in your mind. Things like wishing you were back in Portland, fear, wishing you were back in Portland . . . Be pleasant even if they stare at you. . . . Damn! Stop feeling sorry for yourself! You've got a right to be here. The fact that Dan wants you here is your right. Where's your guts, Casey? *Gone! Dammit! Gone!*

She was completely unaware of the misery in her eyes when she looked at Aunt Bea.

"Don't think you're going to get out of helping, Casey. Here's a knife, start cutting on those pies. Cut the little ones in six pieces and the big ones in eight." She moved the pies down the counter. "That's Marge and her five. She's a jewel of a mother. She's training her kids right, too. Can't say as much for Helen. She's too busy golfing."

Casey grabbed onto the knife like a lifeline, relieved to have something to do. Her eyes kept going to the door. Dan said he would be with her. *Oh, hell!* she thought in self-disgust. Why am I being so chicken? It's no big deal!

The porch door slammed and five children tried to come through the kitchen door at the same time.

"Leave the food out on the porch, kids," Aunt Bea called and there was another scramble to get back through the door.

"Thanks, guys." The drill sergeant's voice was softer. "Go on out and play. Stay away from the river and keep your eye on Jayne. When you start the ball game, bring her in, and I'll watch her."

Casey didn't have time to imagine a body to go with the voice talking to the children, still she was surprised when a small woman with short dark hair and a sweet smile came into the kitchen. She was wearing jeans, a checked shirt, and running shoes. Her eyes went straight to Casey and stayed there. They were large and smiling and Casey couldn't possibly do anything but smile back at her.

"You're Casey."

"Course she's Casey," Aunt Bea chuckled. "The minute I laid eyes on her I knew she was the one for Daniel. Wait'll you see the two of them together. Him, so dark, and her, all gold . . . like honey."

Marge came around the counter, a genuine welcome on her face. "I'm Marge, Fred's wife. I'm so glad to meet you, at last. I've been nervous all day." She hugged Casey and pressed her cheek briefly, then stood back smiling.

"You've been nervous?" Casey laughed with pure relief. "I've been about to blow a gasket!"

"Hi, Marge." Dan came in from the porch. "I see you've already met my lady." He put his arm across his sister-in-law's shoulders and she circled his body with hers and gave him a hug.

"Yes, I've met her. How're you doin', Danny?"

"Fine, my little Margie, how about you?" He placed a kiss on her forehead.

"Unhand my woman, boy!"

The man had come in from the living room. He was shorter than Dan but the family resemblance was there in the dark hair and eyes, and the stocky build. His dark hair was threaded with gray and he wore a mustache.

"Darling! I didn't expect you so soon." Marge went to him and raised her face for his kiss. "You didn't go by home and change clothes," she scolded. "Give me your coat. Take off that tie and be comfortable."

"I wanted to look nice when I met Casey," he said in a staged whisper.

"You don't need to look nice for Casey. You belong to me," Marge whispered back.

"And mighty glad that I do." With an arm around his wife he walked over and held out his hand. "I'm Fred."

Casey almost winced at the firm clasp of his hand. "Hello, Fred. Happy to meet you."

"I'm glad this kid's got a woman of his own. He's been loving on mine for years," he said and playfully poked his finger in Dan's chest. Then, "Why hello, Aunt Honey Bea. How are you doing? What did you make for me to eat? I never get anything good to eat at home."

"Hear that, Marge. I'd not cook for him if I was you. You men better get out there and herd them youngsters so us women can get the food out. Helen and her bunch should be coming."

Dan stood close to Casey. "Are you okay, sweetheart?"

"You go on. I'll be fine," she whispered and meant it.

Helen Murdock was a tall, prematurely gray-haired woman, with a large but trim frame and wide hips. She was pleasant when introduced to Casey, but she lacked the warmth of her sister-in-law. Her children were loud and boisterous and plainly adored their Uncle Dan. She announced that Hank would be late and that they should go ahead and eat without him. The sister she had in tow was a younger replica of herself with blond hair and a sallow complexion that Casey knew at a glance was due to the wrong kind of makeup and hair coloring. The woman offered a cold, limp hand and Casey touched it briefly.

Casey floated along on a light cloud of happiness, chiding herself for doubting that Dan's family would be anything but welcoming. The conversation was light, bantering, never serious. They talked of nothing profound or personal. To her surprise, she found herself chatting easily with Fred and the women. Dan played a game of ball with the children and herded them inside to eat. His eyes turned to Casey at every opportunity and when he was near he touched her, caressed her, and in every possible way showed his family he cared about her. It was the warmest, most wonderful feeling Casey had ever experienced.

Only one thing happened to bring reality back in focus. When they were sitting down at the picnic tables on the porch Helen's sister's child refused to sit at the table with the other children. She was a thin, whining child of about six. Her mother tried to make her sit on the bench beside Casey. The child stiffened and scrambled away.

"No! I won't sit by her. One side of her face is all ucky! Her hands are ucky, too!" She stood back and glared at Casey defiantly.

There was total silence.

Casey swallowed hard. She knew her face was aflame. In the quiet that followed the child's outburst her heart pulsed with an acute pain. To make matters worse, the child's mother tried to apologize.

"I'm sorry. Maryann isn't used to seeing anyone . . . ah . . . who is . . . You see she's very sensitive to others and . . ."

"She's so sensitive she needs her bottom spanked," Aunt Bea said from the other end of the table.

"Aunt Bea!" This came from Helen. "She's only a child."

Casey prayed the floor would open up and swallow her. All eyes were riveted to her face. Then pride surfaced. Damn this woman and her illmannered child. She smiled, although her face felt as if it was set in plaster, and resisted the desire to cover her cheek with her hand. Instead she tilted her head to allow the smooth curtain of golden hair to slide forward.

"It's all right," she said to the child's mother through stiff lips.

"I'm sure Maryann will get used to you," the woman said lamely and Casey wanted to hit her. *Shut up!* she screamed silently.

Dan's hand moved across her lap, burrowed between her thighs, and squeezed hard. Casey didn't dare look at him or she would burst into tears and disgrace both of them.

The commotion of serving the children kept the others occupied and Casey managed to get her emotions under control. She held tightly to the hand that lay in her lap until she had to release it so Dan could eat. The meal was bearable because of the constant chatter among Marge, her husband, and Dan. When it was over, the children went back to their play and Casey got up to help Aunt Bea clear the table.

"Sit right there and talk to Marge while she feeds Jayne," Aunt Bea commanded. "Helen and Lucy can help me take care of this."

"I want mama to play with me," Maryann said. Her small face was set stubbornly and her eyes didn't waver as she looked directly at Casey.

"Well . . . I never!" Aunt Bea stood with hands on her ample hips.

"Come on, darling. Sit in here on a stool while mama helps Aunty Bea." Lucy urged the child into the kitchen.

Marge's lips quirked into a smile and her bright eyes sought Fred's. Casey saw the look of understanding pass between them and Fred leaned over and kissed his wife on the lips.

"I know," he whispered. "You're a mean mama. Our kids would never get away with that."

"You better believe it!"

The love between the two of them was obvious to Casey. Dan would be that kind of husband and father if he truly loved the woman he married. The physical attraction he felt for her was undeniable. But love? Was it possible to love so intensely on such short acquaintance? Was it pity, or guilt he was mistaking for love?

Marge and Fred gathered their family together and left after Marge made arrangements to come over and spend the afternoon while Dan was away. Helen was loading her children in a large van when her husband arrived. One by one the children, with the exception of Maryann, came to tell them good-bye. Casey almost burst out laughing when the child peeked from behind her mother and stuck out her tongue. Somehow it eased the tension that clawed at her stomach and she just barely resisted the impulse to poke out her own tongue.

There was much hugging and kissing between Hank and his children before Helen drove away. This confirmed Casey's first impression that the Murdocks were strong family men. She studied Hank as he walked toward them. He was as tall as Dan but not as heavily built. His hair had receded far back from his forehead and he wore large, dark-rimmed glasses.

"Sorry to be so late," he said as he approached them. "There was an accident at the mill and I wanted to wait around and find out how serious it was. The young Franklin boy almost lost a hand." He held out his hand to Casey and smiled, but somehow Casey didn't think the smile quite reached his eyes. "Hello, Casey. I see you survived the thundering herd, as Aunt Bea calls them."

"Oh, yes. I'm not all that fragile."

Dan threw an arm casually across her shoulders. "Come on in, Hank. Aunt Bea saved your supper."

When Hank left an hour later, Casey was convinced he was somewhat less than enthusiastic about her being in his brother's home. He and Dan had sat at the table and talked business. There was a problem with the foreign contract and Dan would have to go to Japan to straighten it out. Casey chatted with Aunt Bea and, after she left to go back through the break in the fence to her own house, Casey wandered into the living room. Later she couldn't remember Dan's older brother directing any conversation to her other than the greeting when he came and "goodnight, Casey" when he left.

Dan closed the door behind his brother and leaned against it.

"Well? How was it?"

"Harrowing."

"Harrowing?"

"Harrowing, as in painful, nerve-racking, and frantic. Until tonight I haven't been in a group where more than three people were related and not close enough to a child to touch one since my car broke down and I had to ride the bus." She wanted to tell him that she loved every minute of it, but she couldn't. "I think I do better on a one-to-one basis . . . me and Aunt Bea . . . me and Marge . . ."

"Me and . . . you. Come here, Clementine." Dan opened his arms and she went into them. He pressed his parted lips to hers. His hands slid up under her sweater and were stopped from going farther by the belt at her waist. "I'm going to have to teach you to dress properly," he muttered. His fingers worked at the buckle and the belt fell to the floor. Caressing the warm flesh of her back he gathered her to him. "Ahhhh . . the back door is bolted. There'll be no interruptions this time. Shall we sit on the couch? I liked what you were doing this evening . . . before we were invaded."

"Dan . . . I don't think—"

His mouth came down hard on hers, stifling her words, a sense of long pent-up restraint being cast aside. He whispered something through the kiss that sounded vaguely like, "don't think." His touch was carrying her beyond reason. When he raised his head and a soft chuckle of triumph escaped him, she stiffened.

"It's too risky." She forced herself away from him and he let her go.

"Too . . . risky?" His voice was a hollow echo.

"I could already be pregnant!" she said desperately.

"You want to have a family, don't you, Casey?" he asked quietly. "Or has seeing my brothers' broods put you off?"

She moved toward the living room and he followed. She knew when he called her Casey his mood was serious. The effect she had wished for was achieved, but now she wasn't so sure she could handle it.

"Of course I want a family some day, but not now. I've got the operations . . ." Her voice trailed away, then came back stronger. "Besides we've nothing concrete to offer a child."

"What the hell do you mean by that? We love each other. We'd make good parents."

"Oh, come out of the clouds, Dan! We can't be sure of that. We don't *really* know each other all that well."

He caught her as they neared the couch and deftly twisted her down on it. His glittering dark eyes were close. She gazed at him blindly, waiting, her own amber eyes fixed on his hard, sensual mouth.

"That's a lie and you know it! You're afraid of commitment."

Once she would have bristled or else run like a rabbit from such a statement. But now her throat felt hot, her legs weak because she knew his will was stronger than hers. She leaned back against the cushions, her head cloudy, waiting. In a moment, unable to resist him, she would by lying in his arms, weak and yielding, her arms around his neck.

"I can understand why you don't want a baby right now, sweetheart. Living here with me and the change in life-style will be a big enough adjustment for you to make all at once." He drew her to him. She looked into his eyes and was shattered by the tenderness she saw there.

"I wish you wouldn't be so good to me," she whispered. "I can't fight against you." She felt a strange slackness in the pit of her stomach.

"I love you, my Guinevere." He put a hand under

her chin and lifted her face to his, kissing her gently, lovingly.

Casey said nothing, not knowing what to say. He had spoken the truth. He sincerely believed he loved her. There had been something infinitely special between them from the first moment they met. Was she crazy? Did she only *want* to think that? She searched his eyes and he smiled gently. It made nothing more important than being with him, now, this minute.

He wrapped her in his arms and pressed her head to his shoulder. "You heard Hank talk about the trouble with the contracts. I'll leave for Japan the day after tomorrow. While I'm gone you can call Dr. Masters at the hospital and he will phone a prescription to the pharmacy here. I won't be able to stay away from you, sweetheart, don't ask me to. The only other thing to do is to get some protection."

"How long will you be gone?"

"Five or six days. You'll be all right here. Aunt Bea is just next door and I heard Marge say she was coming out."

"Are you sure I should stay? I'd rather go home to my apartment," she said hesitantly. "I don't think Hank is too keen on me being here. It's occurred to me that he and Helen had something in mind for you and her sister, Lucy."

"Helen had something in mind. I won't deny it." Casey felt the chuckle in his chest. "Your coming on the scene has put a stop to that, thank God!"

"But Hank?"

"Hank is a 'wait and see' man. He never makes snap decisions. His life is the mill and his kids. I don't mean that his life with Helen isn't happy. She's a good wife to him because she asks only for time for her committee meetings and golf and makes few demands on his time, leaving him time for his hobby . . . work. He's a workaholic. Fred and I see the mill as a challenge, a way to make a living. We get satisfaction out of providing jobs so other men can make a living, too, but the mill isn't our whole life as it is Hank's." She couldn't see his face, but she knew it was serious. "Fred's life is Marge. He loves her to distraction. Always has. I don't know if he could take it if anything happened to her."

Casey raised her head cautiously. "You sound as if something could happen to her."

"She hasn't been . . . well. It was her idea to have five children. She's the proverbial mother."

"She looks healthy," Casey said, seeing in her mind's eye the laughing dark eyes and cheerful smile.

"I think she is, now. I'm glad you got on well with her. She's sort of special to me." He shifted Casey so that she lay across his lap. "Enough of that. Isn't it a good feeling to be alone here in our house?"

"You mean you like it better than in the wagon or on the barge, or at Camelot?" she teased and rubbed her fingertips lightly across his cheek.

"I like it better because it's now," he growled and kissed her nose before setting his lips against her mouth. His kiss was urgent from the beginning, a demanding heat in the movement of his mouth, a flaring hunger, which she met with a hunger of her own. His hands traveled softly down her body. "I love touching your warm nakedness," he whispered. "It's only then that I feel you truly give yourself to me. Let's go to bed, sweetheart." As his mouth moved over her face, pressing gently against the scar, she felt the urgency growing inside them both.

"Dan, darling, we shouldn't . . ."

"When are you due?" His whisper came thickly against her lips.

"Three days. But . . ."

"Let's chance it, sweetheart." His heart was pounding against hers and there was a fine dew of perspiration on his forehead. "Unless you want me to . . ."

She rolled off his lap and got to her feet. Her arms encircled his waist when he stood beside her. "No," she said against his neck. "Give me a few minutes."

In her room she stood with her back to the door. "He's right to want to get married," she said aloud. "He'll make a marvelous husband and father. It's *me* I have doubts about. Will I be miserable if the marriage is less than perfect?" She took her nightgown from the drawer, went into the bathroom, and shut and locked the door. *He deserves so much more than a woman who has serious doubts a marriage will work, a woman who has been less than honest with him about the accident. Will he realize what he feels for me is pity when he learns that he was not responsible for the scars on my body? Oh, damn! I love him so much I don't think I could bear to see revulsion on his face.*

In the mirror her eyes were wide and darkly brilliant, and the girl she saw reflected there looked like a stranger. She had known this new Casey with the scarred face and dark circles beneath her eyes for only a short time. Abruptly she turned away and forced herself to be calm. She slipped into her prim nightgown and brushed her hair, arranging it to cover the scar, and dabbed cologne on her wrists and temples. She went back into the bedroom half expecting Dan to be there, but the room was empty. After turning out all the lights except the one on the table beside the bed, she turned back the covers and slipped between the smooth sheets.

When he came, it was silently. The door was pushed back and he was there in the doorway. All he was wearing was brief, white jockey shorts, the white a startling contrast against his sun-bronzed body. He leaned casually against the door, his dark eyes on her face. She watched him walk toward her in all his natural splendor. He was an extraordinarily masculine man; broad shoulders, trim hips, long legs.

He sat down next to her on the bed, and kissed her.

"You're a beautiful man." She said it very softly, and ran her palm over his cheek. "You've showered and shaved and you smell good, too."

He smiled at her in amusement and bent forward for a rapid kiss. "I want everything to be just right when I make love to m'lady."

She slipped her arms about his neck. "Well, what are you waiting for? Get on with it, my man."

He took her hands and held them against his chest and looked down at her with a smile in his deep, dark eyes. Then he stood, hooked his thumbs in the top of his shorts, pushed them down, and stepped out of them. He stood before her, proud and indifferent to his nakedness, walked to the other side of the bed and lifted the covers.

Casey swallowed the large lump blocking her throat and fumbled with the switch on the lamp, finally succeeding in plunging the room into darkness. She felt Dan hesitate, then he was moving across the bed toward her. His arm slipped beneath her and pulled her over until she lay against his chest. His hand worked at the gown until he could reach her bare buttocks and knead them gently with his flattened palm.

"Why did you do that?" He was nuzzling the side of her neck under her hair. The tip of his tongue stroked the soft skin beneath her ear.

"What?" she quavered. It was hard to articulate

anything in this position. He had spread his thighs and she lay between them.

"Did the sight of my nakedness bother you?" His voice was barely a whisper.

"No." She sought his lips so she wouldn't have to say more.

His lips settled on her mouth and he kissed her long and tenderly while his fingers stroked the softness of her inner thighs. Then his mouth trailed across her cheek to her ear and teased it with darting tongue and soft, warm breath. His hands worked the gown up and over her head and he flung it from him almost angrily.

"I hate that thing!" She lay on top of him, her breasts nestled firmly against the dark hair of his chest, her flat belly against him, the cradle of her femininity tightly pressed against the mass of dark hair at his groin. "I want to see you when I make love to you."

Fear stabbed through Casey causing her to stiffen. *There was reproach in his voice!* "No . . . not tonight. Please, darling."

His arms and his legs folded about her, holding her closer. He was still and silent for a long while, then he rolled over and pinned her beneath him. She closed her eyes tightly, her heart hammering with dread. *Would he flip on the light?* With a strength garnered from panic she locked her arms about his neck and pressed her mouth urgently to his, kissing him with all the passion born from the thought of dying desire if he should turn on the light and see her scarred body.

"You know it can't always be like this," he whispered while stroking her temple with his fingers. "I want unconditional acceptance, which means you love me enough to allow me full access to your body and mind. I want us to be truly one, my Clementine, with no secrets between us . . . ever."

Casey didn't speak, couldn't speak. Tears coursed

from the corners of her eyes till they disappeared in the hair above her ears. Dan's finger stopped one rivulet and his lips sipped the tears from her other cheek.

"Sweetheart?" he whispered solicitously. "Don't cry. It's not a problem we have to solve tonight. And it's not an insurmountable one anyway." He rolled with her again and brought her up to lay across his chest. "You're always on the defensive, my love. But never mind that, now. We'll talk about it when I come back."

The pain in Casey's breast swelled with alarming intensity. "Give me just a little time," she said shakily. Silently, she cried, Oh, Lord, will this be the last time I'll be with him like this? In a frenzy she began to kiss and caress him.

When he could free his mouth, he laughed softly. "Don't rush the fence, my Cleopatra of the Nile, my little sexpot." His lips covered hers lightly, his tongue caressing the corners of her mouth with a velvet touch. "The best sex is soft and sweet and long. We have the night and I intend to use it all making soft, sweet love to you."

Eleven

Dan turned to look at her in the silence of the big car. For a moment there was worry in his eyes. "You'll be all right, won't you?"

Casey nodded quietly, and then let out a small sigh. Her eyes found his. "I'll be fine, but I'll miss you terribly."

"I'll miss you, too."

"Will they take you to one of those Geisha houses?" There was a teasing sparkle in her eyes as she studied his profile.

"Would you mind?" He grinned in that endearing way of his.

"I'd mind . . . like hell!"

He laughed happily and reached for her hand as he took the turn off for the airport where he would board the commuter plane for Portland.

"Aunt Bea will look after you. If you find you don't want to stay alone at night, she'll come over and sleep in mother's room."

"I know. She told me. I won't mind being alone.

Besides, I'll have Sadie. She'd bark if someone strange came around."

"She'd do that all right. I told Fred to stop by a few times."

Casey looked at him in surprise. "Why'd you do that?"

"Because I want to make sure you're okay, my Guinevere."

"Thanks for your concern, but it seems silly to bother Fred. You'll only be gone five days."

"I'm sure they'll be the longest five days of my life." He pulled her hand to his lips and gently kissed the tips of her fingers. "I wish you were going with me."

"So do I."

He pulled into the parking. "Coming in?"

She shook her head. "I hate public good-byes." She was terrified she would break down and cry when he left her. "What time does your plane leave?"

"I'll have about an hour after I get to the Portland airport."

"Don't work too hard? And . . . you'll take care of yourself?"

He smiled at her tenderly. "I won't and . . . I will."

He put his arm around her and held her close. She put her arms around him and squeezed her eyes shut. She had come to depend on him so much during the last few weeks. She needed him more than he could possibly know.

"Don't forget that I love you, Clementine."

"I love you, too."

"You're sure you can find your way back home?" She nodded and he kissed her hard. "It's time to go."

He got out of the car and took his case from the back seat. Casey moved over under the wheel. He leaned through the car window for another quick kiss.

"I love you." She wasn't sure she had even said it aloud.

He turned and strode into the terminal without a backward glance or a wave. She watched until he disappeared, her own words, *I love you,* echoing in her head. She sat there until the small blue plane took off, circled the airfield, and headed northwest.

Casey spent a peaceful afternoon in the small upstairs room with her sewing machine. She had found a knit shirt in Dan's closet and cut a newspaper pattern from it. She giggled when she pulled the fabric with the broad stripes from among her supply of materials and for just a second considered making the shirt from it. But she wanted this shirt to be special so she chose a length of colonial blue knit. The pieces she cut were large and easy to work with and the shirt went together like a dream. The garment was completed, except for the white collar she would add later, when she heard Sadie bark, and a car door slam.

She peeked out the window, then ran down to open the door.

"Hi, Fred."

"How'er ya doin' Casey?"

"Fine. How's Marge?"

"Fine." He laughed. "Now we've got the preliminaries over with, what've you got cold to drink?"

Casey laughed and waved him into the kitchen. She liked Fred. This was his third visit since Dan had been gone and they went through the same singsong monologue each time he arrived.

"How about a beer?"

"Sounds great. Marge said to tell you she would be over tomorrow. It's nursery school day for Jayne."

Casey took a frosted glass from the freezer and a can of beer from the refrigerator. "You don't need to come by here every day, Fred. I'm doing just fine."

"No trouble, Casey. It's just a little out of my way." He lowered his voice to a conspiratorial whisper. "It's the least I can do for my little brother."

"Little?" She laughed with him and sat down.

He suddenly sobered. "Do you love him, Casey? Really love him?" It was the first personal question he had asked her.

She looked at him for a long moment. "Yes. I do," she said quietly.

Gently, he reached over and patted her hand. "I'm glad. I'm so damn glad!" He gulped his drink and got to his feet. "I can't stop by tomorrow. I'll be down south at the logging camp all day." She walked with him through the house. At the door he grinned at her and the grin was so much like Dan's that her heart skipped a beat. "He called today. Said to tell you he misses you."

"Fred! For Pete's sake! Why didn't you tell me that right away? Did he say the work was going well?"

"Oh, yes. He'll be leaving on schedule. Should be in day after tomorrow."

"He said he would call from Portland and let me know what time to pick him up." Casey thought as she stood on the steps and watched Dan's brother drive away. A couple of days and Dan would be back! What happened after that would just have to happen; she couldn't live with this sense of dread any longer.

When Marge came the next day Casey showed her the shirt. "Do you think he'll like it?"

"He'll love it, if for no other reason than you made it for him. He's really gone on you, Casey. I never imagined Dan would fall so hard, but I should've realized he would when he met the right woman. He and my Fred are so much alike."

"We've known each other for such a short time. I'm not convinced that what Dan feels for me is love. I wake up at night and think I'm living in a dream world. With all the women he has known, it's unreal that he would have chosen me." Casey's eyes took on a strange far-away look.

"Is something wrong?"

"Wrong?" Casey's mind jerked to the present. "Only almost everything. How can you look at me and ask?"

Marge twisted her coffee mug around and around in her hands. "I could have clobbered that spoiled child of Lucy's the other night. I wanted to say something, but decided the least said the better."

"I was mortified at first," Casey admitted. "But you can't blame the child. I never really thought I was vain, but I guess I am. It does something to my self-esteem knowing that some people find my looks offensive."

"Because the scar is on *your* face it seems to you bigger than life. Not one of my children mentioned it. I don't think they even noticed. And Casey . . . you only have to live with it for a few months. Dan said the plastic surgeon can remove it almost completely." Marge looked at her hopefully.

Casey shook her head. "It isn't only my face. I'm one solid scar from my shoulders to my knees. Scars that can't be fixed. My breast is all lopsided . . . and ugly. My stomach and thighs are covered with puckers and ridges. No man, not even Dan, who thinks he loves me, could think of seduction when he looks at my body." Tears, that had come so easy since the accident, filled her eyes.

The two looked at each other with despair. "You're wrong if you think it will matter to Dan. If a man really loves you he'll settle for less than perfection. Real love is quiet understanding, mutual confidence, sharing, and forgiving. Love makes all sorts of allowances for human frailties and weaknesses."

"Thank you for saying that," Casey said quietly, the despair still in her eyes. "It's a problem I'll have to face as soon as Dan returns. I shouldn't have let the relationship develop, but somehow it did." Casey stared into her cup.

"Give Dan a chance. Believe me, Casey, the Murdock men are strong. When they love, it's with all their hearts." Marge's eyes pleaded with her; they were filled with concern.

"Dan is a very . . . physical man! Oh, Marge, you should see my breast and you'd understand!" She looked white and shaken. This was the first time she had voiced her despair.

"And . . . you should see where mine . . . was." The words came out quietly and there was not a hint of impatience in her voice.

"Was?" Casey looked shocked. Then, "Oh, Marge!"

"Don't look so horrified. I had a mastectomy four years ago. Also my child-bearing years are over. But the sexual part of our lives has never been better." Her dark eyes took on a shine. "I was worried at first, but Fred said our love made up for any missing parts either of us would ever have. We are closer than we've ever been, because we don't take each other for granted anymore."

"What can I say?" Casey smiled through her tears. She was crying for Marge now, not for herself.

"Don't say anything." Marge looked at her watch. "Gotta go pick up Jayne. My vacation is over for the week." She rinsed her coffee cup and turned it upside down on the drain board. Her eyes were twinkling. "I've got my heart set on having you for a sister-in-law. Don't you dare let me down!"

Later Casey walked over to Aunt Bea's. The two women had a quiet dinner and Casey returned to the house before dark. Tomorrow Dan would be back. The thought pounded through her head. When I get back we'll talk about it, he had said. Imprisoned in her thoughts she locked the doors and went upstairs to her bedroom, and lay on the bed she had shared with Dan. Long before the evening was over she was convinced that once he returned and they had their talk the relationship would be over. Regardless, she reasoned, I can't go on like this much longer. She rehearsed what she was going to say, schooled herself for a rejection, and mentally planned for the shop that would be her sole source of support once the operations were over.

Her troubled mind refused to allow her a restful sleep and she rose tired and listless, a sense of tragedy consuming her so that she wanted to weep. She moved about the quiet house in robe and slippers; fed Sadie, replaced magazines, and picked up newspapers.

When the car skidded to a halt on the front drive and two doors were slammed shut almost simultaneously Casey hurried to the door to look out. Fred and Aunt Bea were coming up the steps. She quickly opened the door.

"Oh, Casey . . ." Aunt Bea gasped.

Casey almost froze. "Aunt Bea . . . Fred . . . what is it?"

Fred stood there, his eyes full of fear. "Dan's plane has been hijacked. There's a crazy on board with an explosive strapped to his waist and he says he'll blow up the plane if it doesn't take him to Cuba."

Casey sagged and gripped the wood frame of the doorway. "A bomb . . . on Dan's plane?"

"It was on the morning news and I checked Dan's flight and made sure he was on the plane before I came over."

"Can't they just fly to Cuba and let the crackpot

off?" Aunt Bea looked years older this morning. Her cheeks were wet with tears and her usually neat hair was in disarray.

"They don't have the fuel to fly to Cuba. They've *got* to land and he swears he'll blow up the plane if they attempt it."

Casey felt sick. Aunt Bea saw her sway and rushed forward to put a strong arm about her waist. "Are you sure it isn't a hoax?" Her voice sounded as if it came through a tunnel.

"It isn't a hoax, Casey," Fred said firmly. "Damn . . . damn the lunatics of this world!" He pounded his fist against the door.

Casey fought for control and lurched toward the stairs. "I'm going to Portland. I've got to be there. . . ."

"Stay here, Casey. Fred's going. He'll call as soon as he finds out anything." Aunt Bea hurried up the stairs behind her. "You'll be better off waiting here. There won't be a thing that you can do in Portland."

"I'm going! I'm going!" Casey turned on the stairs. "Fred . . .?"

"There's a plane waiting for me at the airport. They're diverting all aircraft from the International Airport, but we can land at a small private field and drive over. I figure you have a right to be there, so hurry."

During the short flight to Portland Casey's mind never seemed to stop its constant whirring: *You're my Guinevere . . . I'm your Lancelot . . . we made love in the back of the wagon coming across the plains, my Clementine. We've been together for at least a thousand years, we'll make it another fifty.* Was this the end of their time together in this life? Would they meet again in the distant future on some far away planet or on a space station riding high above the earth? Fear closed like a wall around her. She shut her eyes against the thought of not seeing him again and saw his image on the screen of her mind; broad shouldered, masculine, standing in her bedroom door, his thumbs hooked in the elastic top of his jockey shorts. In that moment she experienced such a surge of despair that reason almost left her.

Casey climbed down out of the aircraft and walked on stiff legs to the car waiting to take them to International Airport. The driver told them the big Boeing 747 was within thirty-five minutes of the airport. The hijacker boarded the plane at Honolulu, and had immediately made his demands known to the pilot.

"That's all I can tell you. The officials are being pretty closemouthed."

The name Murdock was their passport through the checkpoints set up at access roads. The police had thrown up a tight network around the landing field, allowing only authorized personnel and emergency vehicles to pass. They got out of the car and passed through the crowd of Army personnel, uniformed police, TV cameramen, and press people. They were taken to a room set aside for the frightened relatives of the passengers aboard the plane. Worried looking airline officials were evasive when Fred questioned them for news. No one wanted to commit himself, or raise false hopes. A TV monitoring screen had been set up in the lounge and people sat quietly watching, waiting, praying, weeping softly. A serving cart passed among them passing out coffee and cold drinks. Casey silently shook her head when offered a drink, but Fred reached for two paper cups of cola and pressed one into her hand.

"You're going to fall apart if you don't let go a little. Drink this. It's something to do."

Feeling panic stricken, Casey could hear her own heart pounding in her ears. During the whole agonizing flight from Bend and the ride to the airport she hadn't thought even once about her face, or the fact that she hadn't brought her head scarf. Her hand went to her cheek, now, and she fingered the rough skin, not knowing or caring that she was drawing attention to it. Then a crisp voice flowed into the room and a tremor went through her as she sat forward to concentrate on the screen.

"The Channel Eight News crew are now set up at International Airport to bring you the latest information about the hijacked Boeing 747 with one hundred and forty-three passengers and crew aboard. It has been confirmed that several notable passengers are aboard, including Daniel Murdock, well-known international rugby player, and Claudia Wells, screen and stage star. The airport here in Portland is locked in and all planes are being diverted to Vancouver or Seattle. Our latest information being relayed from the control tower is that the pilot is stalling to allow as much fuel as possible to be consumed in order to convince the hijacker that the plane must land at Portland to refuel. Stay tuned to this channel. Our camera crews have set up on the runway and you will be first, through Channel Eight News, to see the plane land . . . that is if it lands."

A hum of voices rose when the face of the announcer disappeared from the screen and the camera began scanning the sky. Casey slumped back despairingly.

A woman began to weep.

Casey wasn't aware she had grasped Fred's hand until he gently disengaged it. "I'll go see what I can find out."

She nodded. She had become a robot, an automated body without a mind; functioning, but she couldn't understand why. All she could think of was Dan—big, gentle, laughing.

There was a feverish quality about the way the waiting relatives stood in small groups and held on to each other. The room was quiet except for the voice on the monitor repeating things about mobile cameras, security positions, making small talk in order to stay on the air until the plane arrived. Each time the news commentator came on all eyes swiveled in the direction of the screen.

"We have a news brief just relayed from the communications tower. The hijacker has agreed to allow the plane to land. He has also agreed to allow the women and children to leave the plane. He is still determined, however, to destroy the aircraft if it is not refueled and allowed to take off. Stay tuned to Channel Eight News."

Fred slipped into the seat beside her and put an arm around her shoulders. "I called Marge and told her to watch the news. She said it's on the national and she's seeing what we're seeing."

A gabble of voices broke out and people rushed for the windows. "There it is! It's coming in."

Casey heard the roar of the jets and saw the huge, blue and silver plane swoop low out of the clear sky and aim for the long runway. She whispered a feverent prayer as the landing wheels touched down, bounced softly, and rushed down the stretch of concrete. Her heart was beating, *darling, darling, darling.* The plane slowed to a crawl, turned, and taxied to the far end of the field. The people in the room stood almost spellbound at the windows and watched.

A vehicle with a lone man standing in the back with his arms held high above his head drove slowly toward the plane. The voice of the commentator filled the room.

"The officer is trying to persuade the hijacker to allow him to bring out disembarking equipment so the women and children may leave the plane. We'll know if he succeeds in just a few minutes."

For a long while following this announcement, there was silence. Visible strain and a tremor of fresh panic rippled among the waiting people.

"The bastard could blow up the plane at any time," a middle-aged man with a red face and a large belly that hung over his belt commented.

The remark caused a young woman to bury her face in her hands and burst into tears.

Fred moved over beside the man. "Knock it off!" he said angrily. "We've got enough to deal with without you spelling it out."

Casey scarcely heard the announcer's voice when he explained excitedly that the door of the plane was open and the disembarking equipment was in place. She could see all of this for herself. A gasp of relief came from behind her when a woman leading a small child came down the steps and ran toward the terminal building. As the woman left the plane people in the lounge, some crying with relief, hurried down the corridor to meet them.

Casey kept her eyes riveted to the door, hoping beyond hope that when the last of the women had disembarked the men would start filing out, but it didn't happen. The portable stairway was moved away and the door closed. The common bond of fear and dread among the less than two dozen people left in the lounge kept them silent. Casey felt as if all the air in the room had been sucked out; it was difficult to think, to see, to breathe. She thought for a moment that she would be sick, but she swallowed repeatedly and went on standing beside the window, watching the closed door of the plane.

A close-up of the commentator, holding a fist full of notes, appeared on the monitor. Casey almost dreaded hearing what he would have to say. The camera moved back to bring in the image of a young woman standing beside him.

"The lady with me is Miss Claudia Wells, star of the broadway hit, *Dawn of Passion*. According to Miss Wells, the man responsible for talking the hijacker into letting the women and children leave the plane was Dan Murdock, well-known rugby player. Can you tell us, Miss Wells, how you felt when you were told the plane was being hijacked?"

The camera moved in close. "Scared! Damn scared! If it hadn't been for Dan we would have all panicked. He was marvelous. So calm and practical about the whole thing. I promised him I'd wait . . ."

"Sorry to interrupt, Miss Wells, but I have news. Great news! The hijacker has been disarmed! I repeat. The hijacker has been disarmed! The door of the plane is open and the steps are being put in place. The suspense has been heavy, but it's all over, now. The pilot has radioed that Dan Murdock was able to jerk the fuses from the dynamite after he overpowered the man, who was becoming increasingly agitated. It was feared he was merely waiting for the plane to be airborne before he exploded the bomb."

Casey turned and leaned her head weakly against Fred's shoulder, still unable to believe the nightmare was over.

"Oh, God! Oh, God! I was so scared!" Fred repeated the words over and over.

She clung to his hand. "It's really over?" Her voice was shaky.

"It's over!" Fred laughed with relief. "Will you be all right? I'll go down and bring him up here when they release him. I imagine he'll have some questions to answer."

"I'll be fine."

Casey felt fatigue wash over her like a wave of cement. She stood slumped against the wall. Her eyes went back to the monitor and her ears picked up the newscaster's voice.

"Dan Murdock is a member of the well-known Murdock family who have been prominent in the lumber business since their grandfather, Silas Murdock, started the mill back in the eighteen seventies. His brother was seen coming into the terminal earlier with a young woman who is presumably Dan Murdock's fiancée."

Suddenly Casey's face appeared on the screen. She gasped and turned to see a portable TV camera moving in for a closeup. Her frantic eyes caught her image again. That couldn't be her? Her hair was disheveled and pulled back. The side of her face with the horrible scar was on the screen! She looked ravaged!

"The young woman you see on the screen hasn't identified herself, but she was the one who was seen coming into . . ."

"No! No!" Casey held her hand out as if to ward off a blow. When the camera kept coming toward her, she broke and ran, rushing by the cameraman and almost upsetting him. The shock of seeing her scarred face on the screen put a knot in her chest and a lump in her throat. She couldn't seem to move her feet fast enough to get away, so she concentrated on putting one before the other like a machine until she reached the drive and hailed a taxi.

Twelve

Casey closed the door to her apartment and leaned against it, distracted, for a moment, by the pain in her chest, the result of running up the stairway after she had shoved a large bill into the hands of the grateful cab driver. *Are you all right, lady? Are you all right, lady?* His words echoed in her head and now she answered them aloud.

"No, dammit! I'm not all right! I'll never be all right again!"

With an effort she pushed herself away from the door and went into the bathroom. The face that looked back at her from the mirror above the sink was as pale as the white wall behind her head. She wet a cloth, held it to her face, and breathed deeply. She didn't want to be sick.

The shock of seeing herself on the TV screen had brought all her doubts and fears back into focus. Lost to her were the moments of relief and hope after Marge had told her about her mastectomy. Now she remembered that nothing had changed. To have waited in the lounge for Dan, further inhibited by the presence of Claudia Wells, would have been the ultimate humiliation.

Leaving her clothes in a pile on the bathroom floor, Casey stepped into the shower and turned the water on full force. Her knees were quivering and she held tightly to the faucets for support. She stood for a long while beneath the sharp spray, allowing the water to plaster her hair to her head, fill her eyes and her mouth, wash over her scarred body. Her head throbbed, her neck and shoulders ached. Voices, faces, the pandemonium at the airport, crowded into her head and panic tore at her heart in a way she found almost unbearable. When the water turned icy cold she turned it off and reached for the faded terry cloth robe that hung behind the door.

Common sense told her that the weakness in her knees was party due to her empty stomach. She had eaten very little the night before and nothing at all today. With her hair hanging in strings and dripping wet, she went to the kitchen and opened the refrigerator, looked inside, and closed it again. Was her mind going bad? She and Judy had cleaned it out before they went to the coast! In the cupboard she found a can of tuna fish, opened it, and stood with her back to the counter eating out of the can.

She felt a sudden pang of guilt for leaving Fred without a word after he had been so understanding and bringing her with him to Portland, but she wasn't sorry she had left when she did. What had ever possessed her to go to the airport in the first place?

Dan is the hero of the day, she thought with pride. He will be interviewed and photographed. His face will be on every newscast, she thought miserably. I won't dare watch! I can't watch him with Claudia Wells beside him. She set the partially eaten can of tuna on the counter because she knew she'd be unable to get another bite of food down her throat. Misery, loneliness, jealousy washed over her.

The rasp of the kay in the apartment door startled her and brought her to full awareness, causing her heart to shift into high gear. She stood on stiffened legs in the middle of the room and watched with fascination as the chain on the nightlock stretched taut. She heard a muffled curse.

Dan!

"Open this damned door, Casey!"

Casey! He was very angry! Feeling more panic stricken than she ever had in her life, and almost completely breathless, she scraped up enough courage to say: "I don't want to see you. Go away and leave me alone."

"Are you going to open the door or am I going to break it down?" The tone of his voice savaged her, sending a shiver of dread down her spine. "Answer me, damn you!" He jerked out the words in a voice she had never heard before. "I don't want to cause a scene, but I will if you don't open the door."

Casey stood glued to the floor, incapable of replying. There was silence on the other side of the door. *Was he leaving?* She believed he was when the pressure of the chain relaxed.

Bang! He had kicked the door! The wood holding the chain splintered, but held. Oh, my God! She screamed silently. Someone will call the police! She had time for only that one thought before the second blow ripped the chain from the door and sent it crashing back against the wall.

Dan stood glaring at her. His bulk filled the doorway, his face rigid with anger. His hands clenched and unclenched as if he wanted to hit her. He looked like a caged tiger, ready to spring.

"What in the hell are you trying to do to me?" He dropped the words into the quiet like a bomb. He waited a moment and when Casey didn't answer, he slammed the door shut. "Damn you! You've turned my life upside down!" He looked as if he hated her.

Casey couldn't think, couldn't feel, couldn't move. Her words when they came were wooden and the voice didn't sound like her voice. "I don't want you here."

"I don't give a damn what you want!" he shouted and moved into the room to glare down at her. "I won't be treated like some adolescent who has a puppy love crush on you. I've been patient, knowing the accident was a shock to your nervous system, but you can no longer use that as an excuse for your indecisive behavior toward me!" His rage increased with every word. "Running away from Fred at the airport was thoughtless and inconsiderate. You scared the hell out of both of us. If I hadn't been sure you would come here I'd have called the police. I've had one hell of a day, lady. You running off in a snit was not the least of it!" There was a kind of desperation in the jerky way he spoke.

"I wasn't . . ."

"Don't give me any of your half-ass excuses," he snarled.

She stared at him. His angry dark eyes held hers like a magnet.

"I don't have to give you any excuses at all." Her own anger flared. "You don't own me. This isn't the Dark Ages, Sir Lancelot!" Her eyes flashed into his.

"It's a good thing for you, *m'lady*, that it isn't." There was cold sarcasm in his tone.

She moved, heading for the bedroom. He stepped in front of her. "Get out of my apartment, Dan," she said coolly.

"This is my apartment. I paid the rent," he said cruelly.

"Then I'll leave."

"You'll do nothing of the kind. You'll stay right here." His voice was as quiet and as solid as steel.

"I don't have to!" She was shouting at him now. "I don't have to stay here. I just want to be left alone."

"So you can wallow in self-pity? You're the only beautiful woman in the world who is scarred! Oh, poor Casey!"

"Shut up! Shut up!" she shrieked. Tears were running down her face, but she didn't know it. "Do you want to take my pride and trample it? Is that what you want?" Her eyes were bright as stars and her mouth quivered as she spoke. "I can turn you off damn quick. I can send you running out of here like a scared rabbit." She looked at him with disappointment and pain in her eyes and in every line of her face. Frantic fingers worked at the belt at her waist. She flung the robe open, shoved it back and let it fall to the floor. She stood naked before him. Her hands went to her wet hair and she gathered it in a tight bunch at the top of her head, exposing the ugliness of her scarred face and ear.

"Look at me! Look . . . at . . . me!" She shouted the words and spaced them to give them emphasis. She turned her body from side to side to give him a full view of her distorted breast and the scars that crisscrossed her body. Her feverish, tear-filled eyes clung to his, her face was rigid with anguish. "Look! You wanted to see me when we made love. Now's your chance. Look! Look!" Words popped out of her mouth as if she had no control over them. "Now . . . aren't you glad I made you wait to see the sideshow in broad daylight?" Her voice had risen to a hysterical pitch even though sobs constricted her throat. The words came out jerkily and her voice dripped with desperation.

Dan had been stunned into silence. Now he exploded into action. "Sweetheart . . . why are you doing this to yourself?" He tried to reach out for her, but she knocked his hands away.

"Here I am in living color! What you see is what you get, folks!" She pivoted on her toes. "Wouldn't you rather have this beside you on the TV screen than . . . Miss Claudia Wells?" she taunted. She was beginning to feel lightheaded.

"Casey! Stop it!" Dan's eyes glinted like dark fire and the strength of his fingers brought physical pain when he gripped her shoulders.

Suddenly the anger that had kept her going left her. Her knees began to buckle and her mouth crumbled. Her voice choked on a sob and great gulps of tears tore up from her throat and shuddered through her. With a soft groan Dan pulled her into his arms.

"Let it out, sweetheart. Let it all out," he said against the top of her head. "Cry, my Guinevere. Cry and then we'll talk." He held her close, waiting for the storm of tears to spend themselves.

She was exhausted and did nothing to resist him when he lifted her in his arms and carried her to the couch and sat down with her on his lap.

"Sweetheart, I didn't realize how deeply you were hurt. Is this what you've been afraid of? Did you think my love so shallow it would wash away when I saw the scars on your body? I knew they were there, darling. I've seen them. I've touched them. I lay on the table beside you and blood from my body poured into yours while they were sewing you up." His mouth nuzzled at her wet cheek. "The scars on your body aren't important to me. You are! You're all the sweetness and love I've ever wanted. I wanted so much to touch your breast and to let you know that it didn't matter to me that it wasn't perfect like your other one. Sshhh . . . don't cry, my Clementine."

But she did. She cried with her mouth open against his soft shirt. He smoothed her hair, crooned to her, and traced his mouth along the side of her scarred face.

"Don't grieve, dear love. This will be gone in a few months and there will be no one to see the rest of you, but me." He rocked her in his arms. "Now that I know what's bothering you, we can work it out."

"But . . . there's more! The accident wasn't your fault." She gulped back the sobs and kept her face hidden against his shirt. "You don't have to feel guilty."

"Guilty?" he repeated against her ear. "Who in the hell says I feel guilty?" Casey didn't answer, as fresh sobs shook her. "I don't feel guilty because I ran into the back of your car. It was an unfortunate accident. One that could have been avoided if you'd had taillights on your car. I had your car towed to the nearest service station and the man told me he had taken out the fuse because the lights didn't work. He didn't have one to replace it and you decided to risk going home without rear lights. I don't feel guilty about the accident, except the part about being glad it happened. I can't help being glad, because it brought you into my life. We were destined to meet, my darling, in just that way."

"You knew I had no taillights that night? Why didn't you say something?"

He cradled her naked body in his arms and tilted her chin so he could place soft kisses on her tear-wet face. "It wasn't important." There was more love welling up in his eyes than she had ever seen, and she felt her heart lift on a cloud of happiness. She wrapped her arms about him. "I love you," he said the words simply and looked deeply into her eyes.

"I love you, too." Her voice was strained and she clung to him. "You're sure?" She still was hesitant to believe. "You're sure that my scars . . ."

"Hush, sweetheart. I wish I had insisted we leave the light on that first night. I thought you were shy with me." He buried his face in the curve of her neck and covered her breast with the palm of his hand. "I want to make love to m'lady, but I need a shower and her hair is wet."

Casey cupped his face with her hands and moved her mouth over his with incredible lightness. "Clementine didn't mind in the least when you made love to her in the back of the wagon, and you hadn't had a bath since we crossed the last river." She nibbled at his lips, felt the trembling in him, and marveled at it. "I love you." Her fingers worked at the buttons on his shirt.

With a quick, happy smile he lifted her off his lap and stood. His hands went to the belt on his pants, but his smiling eyes remained on Casey's flushed face. She stayed close to him, waiting, anxious to be united with him. She had never felt so wild and free. He let his shirt fall to the floor and then his trousers. When, at last, he stood in his white jockey shorts, Casey wrapped her arms about him and plunged her hands into the elastic top. She slid her palms over his taut buttocks, down through the legs to the backs of his thighs.

"No Aunt Bea to come in today," he whispered huskily.

She laughed happily against his chest. "I wanted to do this the other night when you came to my room. I love the feel of your skin and your chest hair against my breast."

"I love the feel of you, too," he rasped in an agonized masculine need. "Make love to *me*, darling."

Casey sank to the floor, pulled Dan down beside her, and slid her body over his. She looked into his eyes with a lifetime of love and longing in hers.

"I love you . . . with all my heart. My life was going to be so damned lousy without you. I'll never let you go, now. I'll fight all the Claudia Wellses in the world to keep you with me." Her whispered words came against his lips. She lifted her head and smiled happily down at him, and then settled her mouth on his for a long tender kiss.

His reaction almost startled her. He rolled over with her in his arms and raised his head so he could see her face. She had never hoped to see such love in a man's eyes when they looked at her. She felt truly loved and cherished.

"I love you. I think it would destroy me if I couldn't have you with me. I love everything about you . . . your pride, your honesty, your lovely spirit, your golden eyes I'm going to look into when our bodies join. I love each one of the places on your body that has caused you pain." His lips nuzzled the ear that he hadn't dared to touch before and the breast she had kept hidden from him. He worshipped every inch of her body with his fingertips and his lips.

It was all so much sweeter than before. Casey lay with lids half closed while the stroking of his hands on her skin sent waves of pleasure up and down her spine. He was a gentle, unhurried lover and she welcomed him, now. Welcomed the hard insistent pressure, the flat muscled stomach hard against her softness, welcomed his intrusion into her body with eyes wide, looking into the dark depths of his. She heard the low murmur of love words before he covered her mouth with his, and then she was beyond hearing, beyond everything, except feeling.

The sun crept across the carpet and slanted

across their entwined bodies. Dan propped himself up on an elbow and looked down at her with a face full of love. Her arms encircled him and her hands caressed the smooth skin of his back.

"I was so scared . . . at the airport. I hurt so much, I almost wished I didn't love you so desperately." Her lips moved over his face remembering.

"I was scared, too. I just knew I couldn't let that plane fly me away from you. The poor fool was so strung out he would have gone crazy before we got to Cuba. I was scared, but I was just as scared when I couldn't find you after Fred said you were there." He nipped her on the neck sharply with his teeth. His hands moved to her ribs and he began to tickle her. "You silly, crazy, dopey, ridiculous little jerk! How could you think I could possibly prefer that phony, dressed-up, publicity-seeking movie star to you?"

"Stop it! Don't tickle me . . . you know what will happen!"

"Go ahead," he laughed. "Let it happen." His hands were merciless and he held her to the floor with his powerful thighs and legs.

"Stop! Stop! Please stop! I've been in an accident! I'm injured! I'm sick!" She was giggling uncontrollably.

"Yeah! Yeah! Tell me about it. No? Then tell me what I want to hear and I'll stop."

"I love you . . . love you! You . . . big bully!"

Their laughter filled every corner of the room. She was tangled in his arms and they rolled on the floor into the direct sunlight. It slanted across their bodies, across her scarred breast that Dan bent to kiss.

"You make me . . . sooo happy," he said between kisses. "You make me happy and . . . horny!"

"I'm glad!" She sighed blissfully and gave herself up to his kiss. Sometime later she looked at him with eyes shimmering with love. "Dan . . . do you suppose in our next life we'll be on a space station floating around in space?"

"Could be, princess. But don't worry about it. I'll find you," he said confidently with a big smile.

THE EDITOR'S CORNER

The Editor's Corner is a continuing feature in our LOVESWEPT books. In months to come I'll be giving you information on our plans and tidbits on our authors. Now, though, in introducing our new line, let me tell you how excited we are about LOVESWEPT. And how proud we are to bring to you these fine love stories by some of the very best category romance writers in America! Talented storytellers are the centerpiece of LOVESWEPT. No gimmicks. No tired old formula books. Simply, extraordinary romances that will sometimes make you chuckle, sometimes bring a tear to your eyes, but always give you that warm, special feeling we trust you experienced from the story you've just finished. We think you will be very pleased that we're putting an end to the confusing use of pen names. Our authors are writing under their true names. You'll see each author's picture in her book and learn about her real life in her own words—who she is, how she feels about herself as a person and as a writer.

An interviewer asked me not long ago how I "dealt with all those prima donna authors." I was speechless; and the interviewer looked at me as though he were dealing with a moron. The reason I had no answer for a few moments was that not one of these talented women with whom I have the pleasure to work is even remotely like a prima donna! Each one is as delightful as the romances she writes. Truly, the LOVESWEPT authors make being an editor a joy!

(continued)

Some of the authors you'll encounter in this new line are seasoned pros. You know their work—under a variety of pen names—and you've shown through your purchases of their books that you love them. But you'll find, too, a lot of spanking new names. We are delighted by the fresh talent we've been able to discover and are publishing for the very first time.

And next month you are going to be treated to just such sparkling talent in Billie Green's A TRYST WITH MR. LINCOLN?, LOVESWEPT #7 . . . Helen Conrad's TEMPTATION'S STING, LOVESWEPT #8 . . . and Marie Michael's DECEMBER 32ND . . . AND ALWAYS, LOVESWEPT #9.

A TRYST WITH MR. LINCOLN? by Billie Green is filled with humorous surprises from the moment its heroine, Jiggs O'Malley, awakens in a strange hotel room (with one of the most devastating men I've had the pleasure to come across in paperback pages) . . . through an utterly sensual courtship . . . right until the exciting and heartwarming conclusion.

In **TEMPTATION'S STING,** Helen Conrad has made a lush Samoan island come alive. No piece of travelogue here, but a genuine portrayal of a South Pacific plantation in this day and age and owned by a man any woman would find difficult to turn down! Helen grew up on an island in the Pacific and certainly knows what she is writing about. I think that you're going to love Taylor Winfield's struggle to humanize the spoiled brat heroine Rachel Davidson. And what a delicious struggle it is!

DECEMBER 32ND . . . AND ALWAYS by Marie Michael a story is just as intriguing as its title. Patrissa Hamilton thinks she's "over the hill" approaching her forty-first birthday. Never was there a man who could prove better than Marie Michael's hero Blaise, that a woman was not getting older; she was getting better.

I sincerely hope you've enjoyed these LOVESWEPT romances and will continue to enjoy them. I'm here, as our authors are, to bring you the best in romance reading. We count on two-way communication and welcome your comments and ideas.

With warm good wishes,

Carolyn Nichols

Carolyn Nichols
LOVESWEPT
Bantam Books, Inc.
666 Fifth Avenue
New York, NY 10103